CW00447880

LOVE IN A BOTTLE

ANTAL SZERB

LOVE IN A BOTTLE

SELECTED SHORT STORIES
AND NOVELLAS

Translated from the Hungarian by
Len Rix

PUSHKIN PRESS
LONDON

English translation © Len Rix 2010

First published in Hungarian in 1963 as
Szerelem a palackban © Estate of Antal Szerb

This edition first published in 2010 by
Pushkin Press
12 Chester Terrace
London NW1 4ND

British Library Cataloguing in Publication Data:
A catalogue record for this book is available
from the British Library

ISBN 978 1 906548 28 5

Cover Illustration: *László Moholy-Nagy* Lucia Moholy 1925
© Ford Motor Company Collection The Metropolitan Museum of Art
Art Resource Scala Florence

Frontispiece: Antal Szerb 1935
© Petőfi Literarisches Museum Budapest

Set in 10 on 12 Monotype Baskerville MT
and printed on Munken 90gm in Great Britain by T J International

www.pushkinpress.com

LOVE IN A BOTTLE

Contents

SOME NOTES FROM THE TRANSLATOR   11

LOVE IN A BOTTLE

Love in a Bottle   27
Musings in the Library   45
A Dog Called Madelon   69
The Incurable   81
Fin de Siècle   89
The Duke   115

THE TOWER OF SOLITUDE

The White Magus   139
Ajándok's Betrothal   155
The Tyrant   183

SOME NOTES FROM THE TRANSLATOR

This selection of Antal Szerb's shorter fiction is drawn from a much-loved Hungarian volume entitled *Szerelem a palackban* (*Love in a Bottle*). First compiled in 1947, under a different name, its purpose was to anthologise everything the writer had already published in this genre, together with a variety of texts left in manuscript form. This translation confines itself to work clearly intended by the author for publication and includes only the three most assured of the early novellas. It nonetheless reflects almost the full sweep of his all-too-brief career. Szerb was still a student in 1922 when *Ajándok's Betrothal* was accepted by the influential literary journal *Nyugat*. *The Duke* (1943) was the last such thing he would ever write.

The interest of the early tales, apart from their obvious charm, is of several kinds. They reflect, more directly than the later stories, the intense idealism, both religious and political, that drove the writer in these years, and his efforts to come to terms with his own ingrained romanticism. They also show his rapidly advancing mastery of form, the increasing depth of his characterisation and the first appearance of the distinctively ironic vision that was to become his hallmark. For these reasons they are essential for any overall sense of his developing thought and art. Their grouping at the end of this volume reflects the notion that, for the reader new to this author, they are nonetheless best approached via the experience of his later, more mature work.

The phrase *The Tower of Solitude*, used here as a section heading, refers to a motif that connects all three novellas. Its representative in *Ajándok's Betrothal* is the curious tower-house the young couple dream of building opposite––and in a kind of opposition to—the thriving mill that represents the intense communal life of the village. The heroine's unsociability can doubtless be ascribed to her pampered upbringing, but the childish rebelliousness it provokes leads her into a world of increasingly morbid fantasy. Indeed, from her wilful desertion of the Saint John's Night festivities to her predictable lonely death, her progress prefigures both the central movement and darker aspects of Szerb's 1937 masterpiece *Journey by Moonlight*.

As with the hero of that novel, her ill-fated adventure exposes the limitations of the convivial but self-enclosed social order in which she has been raised. The outlandish *garabonciás* with whom she feels such an instant bond is the very antithesis of its values, its Jungian 'shadow'. And yet, even before his appearance, the lyrical opening vision of a serenely close-knit rural community, regulated by tradition and sanctified by the heavens, has been hedged about with ambiguity. The sacred bonfire and associated betrothal dance are rooted in pagan mystery; beyond the leaping flames the air is filled with dark presences, and, most paradoxically, it is the anarchic *garabonciás* who puts wind in the sails of the becalmed mill. What began as a simple-seeming folkloric idyll has ended as a disturbing and many-sided parable.

The remote astronomical tower in *The White Magus* (1923) seems, at first glance, altogether more benign. The sage's reclusive mountain dwelling is a place of virtuous magic and superhuman knowledge, while the surrounding fields of ice and glittering starscapes signal purity and philosophic detachment. But this noble ideal is counterbalanced by the all-embracing compassion of Princess Zoë, dying of pity for the children of Byzantium. Two ancient and contrasting religious traditions are invoked here. For a writer who had seriously contemplated joining an order, the issues were more than theoretical. Here the debate is resolved through narrative action. It is only in 'dying' that the Magus understands what his lofty isolation has cost him. What adds strangeness and novelty to the argument is the way Szerb presents even the most altruistic love as a form of nostalgia (a theme that will recur) and (as so regularly in these early tales) a passion intimately connected with death.

In *The Tyrant* (also 1923), the Duke prides himself on the "tower of solitude" and "freedom" he has constructed for himself. This time the rebuttal is even more direct. For the idealistic young page, his attitude comes to represent the worst type of blasphemy. The technical achievement in this tale marks a distinct advance on what has gone before. First, there is the teeming psychological hinterland—the powerful, undefined obsession that drives the Duke to groom the page as his own assassin, and the confused desires and yearnings that lead the boy

13

to carry out that role. The narrative moves increasingly inside the characters' heads to focus on their struggles for self-knowledge: both principals strive to clarify their true feelings, and the greater the clarity they achieve the less they seem to understand. Their actions are subject to the same ironic reversals. The more the Duke attempts to subdue his love, the more fiercely it grips him. Every step he takes to alienate the boy intensifies the boy's need for him. The more the pair rationalise their feelings for each other, the more we are made aware of the underlying homoerotic element. Such ironies will constitute the stuff of all Szerb's fiction from now on.

But for all their accomplishment and promise, none of these early offerings can truly be said to carry the distinctive note, that unique compound of warm sympathy, sceptical intelligence and playful irony for which Szerb is best known. That voice first appears in 1934—a milestone year—and is heard in everything he writes from this point on, including his literary-historical studies, his wide-ranging critical essays and even his late historical work *The Queen's Necklace*. It is the voice of a man coming to terms with the baffling and paradoxical nature of the world, and with himself.

To achieve it he had first to leave his beloved Budapest. This was the "self-imposed exile in the cause of greater knowledge" he so wryly describes, which "afflicted a whole generation of young Hungarians between 1924 and 1930". After periods of wandering around Italy, Szerb spent some two or three years in Paris and London, passing his days first in the Bibliothèque National, then in the Reading Room of the British Museum. The former experience is endearingly captured in *Musings in the Library* (1934), the latter in his English-Welsh novel *The Pendragon Legend*, published in the same year.

It was probably in London that he found his true direction. He arrived, of course, deeply versed in several literatures apart from his own, most notably German (Goethe remained a lifelong influence) and French (especially the writers of the Enlightenment and the Pre-Romantic age). But it was the English tradition that spoke to him most intimately. He seems to have read almost everything—his publications already included a study of Blake and a short *History of English Literature*—and, fittingly, the first of the new-style stories is *Fin de Siècle* (1934 again), with its wittily irreverent portraits of Yeats, Wilde, Johnson and Dowson. But his tastes were very broad. Aldous Huxley and P G Wodehouse are discernible influences, while his capacity to parody minor English novelists such as John Buchan, Anthony Hope and a host of others is extraordinary. Wodehouse—whom he translated into Hungarian—might well have encouraged his new-found economy of effect, together with the increasing use of dialogue and pervasive droll humour. The fusion of English understatement and Middle-European irony is of course entirely Szerb's own.

But the new manner is far more than a question of 'voice'. In these stories Szerb found his true material—

the comic confusions of everyday life, even in the orderly life of a scholar. His focus here is on the elementary blindnesses of which we are all capable and the devious workings of the self, with its endless rationalisations and self-deceptions. But however entertaining, this goes far beyond the usual purposes of comedy. The very notion of 'self' as something fixed and stable is revealed as illusory. Typically, the self he most frequently demolishes is his own. The comically inept hero of *Pendragon* was the first of a series of unsparing self-caricatures to be given the treatment, and an equally pitiless self-portraiture, transposed into near-tragic mode, underpins his altogether darker *Journey by Moonlight*. At times these narratives read like exercises in self-mortification—as devised by a latter-day Saint Thomas Loyola with an irrepressible sense of humour. Wryly noting his own follies, the un-heroic hero provides the lucid consciousness through which the action is mediated. It is this lucidity, perhaps even more than the irony in which it results, that marks Szerb's originality and greatness as a writer.

In the short stories, self-directed irony first appears in *A Dog called Madelon*, again from 1934. In this particular tale the fantasy-prone hero persuades himself that he will find "erotic charge" only in a woman with aristocratic credentials ("a truly great passion required three of four centuries' historical background at the very least"). In *Musings in the Library*—1934 again—the criteria are more narrowly intellectual. When, surprisingly, these paragons do manifest themselves, it proves altogether more than that with which the dreamer cares to cope. The subjects of both tales share another characteristic of many of Szerb's heroes, the well-developed incapacity to see what is in front of their noses. Everything is there for the reader to spot exactly where the situation is leading—only the great intellect of the learned scholar fails to notice it. The result is a continual series of surprises and reversals of expectation as the hero stumbles through his private cloud of unknowing. It is all part of Szerb's newly achieved world-view—as is the sense of pathos lurking below the comic surface.

The most genial of all the tales is undoubtedly the title piece, *Love in a Bottle* (1935). Whereas the short stories mentioned so far are best read in connection with *Pendragon*, this one directly anticipates *Journey by Moonlight*. At the core of that novel is the protagonist's obsession with his adolescent femme fatale Éva, a morbid passion characterised by "the exulting humiliation of knowing I was lost for love of her and that she didn't care for me". The 1935 story gives this sentiment wonderfully short shrift. Released by the helpful Klingsor from his devotion to the appalling Guinevere, Lancelot enters a joyous, positive world teeming with possibilities—and finds it "horrible". "What pained him beyond words was that he was no longer miserable."

Szerb's interest in obsession continues in *The Incurable*––yet another case of the writer making sport of a problem with which he was personally only too familiar. It is also a passing reminder of his somewhat amused admiration for the English (by which, like all Hungarians, he means the British), with their absurdly magnificent Empire and other foibles and eccentricities.

Among the many pleasures of these mature-period stories is Szerb's treatment of the minor characters. Even the least of them—from Queen Guinevere all the way down to Maclean's nephew Freddy—seem to have a dynamic inner life of their own, with their personal inner drama running in ironical counterpoint to the main action. This 'roundness' of characterisation reflects Szerb's irrepressible love of life and people. Never an 'angry' or judgemental writer, he views his fellow creatures with benign tolerance and gentle amusement. Even the dragon is "only human, after all".

The very last of these tales, *The Duke* (1943), takes a somewhat different form. Essentially it is a companion piece to his great historical study *The Queen's Necklace*, which had appeared the year before. Faced with mounting persecution on account of his Jewish descent, Szerb had returned to his first love, history. It had become, he tells us, his "country of refuge". In the preface he had identified the Italian Renaissance and the French Revolution as the two seminal periods of European civilisation, and what *The Queen's Necklace* did for eighteenth-century France *The Duke* now does, on a much smaller canvas, for sixteenth-century Italy. Through the "imaginary portrait" of the subject it gives us a cameo of the age, not sparing "the nepotism, the anarchy, the hundred different kinds of decadence" at its core. The resplendent details are constantly undercut by his trademark irony, and the touch is always light, its vast erudition worn with an effortless ease. The final note, with its reference to "the ruin of centuries", is less immediately personal than the intensely elegiac conclusion to *The Queen's Necklace,* but the attitude of all-forgiving, benign acceptance remains undiminished—a remarkable response to the circumstances in which the writer found himself.

Looking, then, at the overall pattern of Szerb's career as a writer, we find both continuity and change. The subject matter and techniques evolve, yet the same deeply sympathetic presence can be felt behind the words. Everything he writes, especially once he has found his voice, comes across as somehow personal, written from the heart—a heart that, for all the lucid intelligence of the mind, seems both intensely in love with life and unusually vulnerable.

That said, we find three broad phases in his writing. The early novellas, as mentioned before, take their origin in the writer's youthful idealism. Having decided against a life in the Church, and with his passionate hopes for a genuinely liberal Hungary brutally dashed, he produced three tales in which his own tendency to all such feeling is submitted to an increasingly sceptical scrutiny—as are those troubling questions of a sexual and spiritual nature unresolved since adolescence. There are other, less accomplished, writings from this period (and earlier) that deal even more directly with those problems, but their interest is chiefly in the light they shed on the struggle.

The next seven or eight years, mostly spent teaching at a commercial secondary school in Budapest, are marked by prolific scholarship—a doctorate on the Hungarian poet Kölcsey, a book on Ibsen, the studies of Blake and the *History of English Literature* mentioned earlier, a work on the Pre-Romantics and monographs on the great Hungarian poets. These achievements, followed by his sojourns in Paris and London, finally brought a mature confidence, along with his new philosophical interest in the nature of the self. Above all they broadened his perspective. When he returned to fiction in 1934 he had found his perfect instrument, that unmistakably personal tone—gentle, playful, genially benevolent, and sharp as a razor. There is a real sense in which everything Szerb wrote before 1937 was, one way or another, a preparation for his acclaimed masterpiece, *Journey by Moonlight*.

But the range of his interests never ceased to broaden. In that same *annus mirabilis* of 1934 his *History of Hungarian Literature* won him public acclaim, resulting in his election to the Presidency of the Hungarian Academy of Writers, a major literary prize (the Baumgarten, twice), and finally, in 1937, and in the teeth of anti-Semitic prejudice, his long-deserved university appointment. The Hungarian study was followed by an even wider-ranging volume, his *History of World Literature* (1941), in which he sought to place the tradition of his own country in the wider European context. It was supported by a lifetime's essays on books and writers from every major Western country. A probable consequence of all this—perhaps accelerated by all that was happening around him— was that his "youthful fascination" with philosophical and psychological matters was steadily giving way to a preoccupation with the grand sweep of human events as distilled through the medium of history. This broader, more 'political' outlook partly distinguishes his third novel *Oliver VII* (1941) from its two predecessors, but its greatest fruit was of course *The Queen's Necklace*. As with young Lytto in *The Tyrant*, Szerb's private cause had been subsumed into a greater one. His very last publication, and one which has enjoyed lasting success, was a compilation of a hundred poems translated from different European languages—his final monument to the civilisation he saw collapsing all around him.

Through all these vicissitudes, the writer's character continued to mellow. Over time his youthful political idealism and religiosity gave way to a more generalised concern with spiritual matters, but the steely insight into human folly that grew out of it never hardened into cynicism. Even as the world darkened around him he retained his good-humoured gentleness, responding with humility and mildness to the blows of fortune, always putting the lives of others before his own. There are many writers who create works of enduring inspiration and charm while behaving no better than the rest of us, or indeed rather worse. The Antal Szerb who was so pointlessly murdered in 1945 is not among them.

LEN RIX   2010

21

PART ONE

LOVE IN A BOTTLE

Short Stories
1934–45

LOVE IN A BOTTLE

Sɪʀ ʟᴀɴᴄᴇʟᴏᴛ, the knight whom blame could never touch, was visiting Chatelmerveil, the castle of Klingsor the magician. They had dined, the host had brought out his finest wines in honour of his distinguished guest, and the two were sitting in the middle of the cavernous Great Hall enjoying a quiet tipple.

"I'm not just saying this out of politeness," said Lancelot, "but I don't remember when I last had such a magnificent wine."

"Home produce," the magician replied modestly. "It's a shame so little of it ever gets drunk. Truly, my dear boy, you can't imagine what a solitary life I lead. No one comes here for years on end. I really do live like a hermit."

"Well, you can hardly be surprised—as I keep telling you—if you practise the black arts. No gentleman dares set foot in the place."

"My magical powers, if you please! I gave up that other boring stuff long ago. There's not the least bit of truth in the things they say about me. Believe me, I always acted with the best of intentions. For example, when I spirited Orilus' bride away, and changed Meliacans into a tortoise when he was about to go off to the Holy Land—and all those tales."

Lancelot was perfectly ready to agree with him. As the evening progressed Klingsor steadily threw off his mood of weary apathy and become ever more congenial. His deep-sunk eyes twinkled with shrewdness and his words sparkled with an old man's wisdom.

"You're a good fellow, my dear Klingsor, I've always said," remarked Lancelot. And he gave the magician a hug.

Beside himself with happiness, Klingsor sent for an even better wine, one he never offered to anyone, and as he poured it into the goblets his hand trembled with emotion. It had a glorious colour. Lancelot rose, his face became solemn—transfigured, even—as he declared:

"Klingsor, the time has come … I raise this cup to my noble lady, Queen Guinevere!"

He downed the entire contents, and stood staring straight ahead for what seemed ages. The magician knew this look. He knew that the moment had come when the amorous knight would either burst into tears and pour his heart out, or seize him by the beard. To pre-empt the latter, and struggling manfully to fight back the dry cough that seemed to be troubling his throat, he asked in a tone of suitable reverence:

"Ah, so the peerless Guinevere is your lady? Perhaps you are on an errand for her right now?"

He knew perfectly well that Guinevere was Lancelot's lady. In those days discretion had not yet been invented, and the most famous loves were peddled by minstrels from country to country. Besides he cared not a whit whether it was Guinevere or Viviane—he no longer had any feeling for women himself.

A fine, unworldly smile played over Lancelot's lips, straining to soar heavenwards, as he replied:

"For these last seven years all my journeying has been in her service. You must surely have heard of some of my doings. True, people love to exaggerate these stories. Right now I'm on my way to slay a dragon. A few days ago, on Saint Michael's Eve, it flew into the Queen's treasury and stole a shoe, one of the pair she was given by her husband, the illustrious Arthur, when he returned from his expedition to Ireland. Some of these dragons are utterly shameless. The Queen has charged me, as her most loyal knight, to recover it. She really wouldn't be happy to see it in anyone else's hand, as I'm sure you will understand."

"So great a love … you must be very happy," Klingsor observed wistfully.

Lancelot was furious.

"Me? Happy? I lug my anguish about with me wherever I go. Sometimes I just lie on the ground and howl. I spend two thirds of my days in active misery, and the other third wondering how I can ever bear it."

"Well, then … I can only assume that the Queen— please don't mind my saying this—doesn't love you."

Lancelot leapt to his feet and clapped his hand on his sword.

"What are you thinking, you old villain, you trader of broken-down horses? How could Queen Guinevere possibly love me when she is King Arthur's wife? She is the most saintly of all the saintly women whose lives have been a reproach to the base nature of our mother Eve."

The magician was about to make a little conciliatory speech, but the long-repressed cough finally erupted. His eyes nearly popped out, and he was on the point of falling out of his chair. Lancelot, fearing he might injure himself, rushed to his aid, pummelled him on the back and tried to comfort him.

"You see, you see," he said. "It seems those scrapes you kept getting into with the jewel of your manhood—before you lost it—clearly weren't enough for you. Take care you don't make any more trouble with your tongue, or you'll end up biting yourself."

The magician recovered soon after. He led Lancelot to his bedchamber and wished him a restful night. At the word 'restful' Lancelot heaved a great sigh. Then he uttered his usual fervent prayer to the heavens to watch over Queen Guinevere, and lay down.

Klingsor was suffering from chronic insomnia at the time. He picked up one of his lighter books of Arabian magic to banish the tedium of the night. But he found little to interest him in what he was reading. Whenever his thoughts turned to Lancelot's fate his eyes filled with tears. Finally he broke down and sobbed. The old magician was a thoroughly good-hearted man—von Eschenbach, like everyone else in the Middle Ages, was quite wrong about him. He had abducted Orilus' bride simply because he knew exactly what sort of ruffian the fellow was. A man who won his lady's hand after his days of knightly battles were over would simply work off his lingering warlike impulses on his wife. He would beat her twice a day, after breakfast and luncheon, and not stop at breaking her wrist. And as for the Meliacans business, he only changed the knight into a tortoise because he knew that if he went to the Holy Land his bride would deceive him with a Jewish stocking merchant.

His heart bled for Lancelot. It seemed inconceivable to him that anyone should suffer so much for love. He too, in his youth, had been something of a ladies' man. But ever since one grim husband had taken his revenge on him in a manner so cruel that even today one cannot write about it without blushing, he had forgotten what love was, and he felt decidedly the better for it.

He spent a long time wondering whether or not he should help his friend. He knew the world would misconstrue whatever he did, and it could all end up with Lancelot seizing him by the beard yet again. But that wasn't enough to stop him. His feelings of pity were far too strong.

He rummaged through his instruments, looking for his magic pincers and the blue spectacles that allowed him to see spirits. Then he took off his shoes and crept into Lancelot's room.

A small candle was burning in the darkness. With the aid of the magic spectacles he could see through the bedclothes, through Lancelot's shirt and skin, and into his body. Looking closely, he was able to follow the mischievous frolickings of the little life spirits as they chased one another up and down the labyrinth of blood vessels. It took him a while to discover which was the Love spirit, but eventually he succeeded. There it sat, astride Lancelot's spine, tickling him with a little feather brush. After a while it grew tired of this game. It wriggled its way adroitly between the folds of the lung and set about squeezing the knight's heart. But it must have got bored with that too, because it then slipped into the aorta, where the flow of blood carried it into the brain. It fiddled about for a while among the convolutions, pulling all sorts of things out of the drawers and then stuffing them back again, got itself tangled up in the network of nerve endings, gave a great yawn and jumped out through Lancelot's mouth onto the bed. There it sat, dangling its legs over the edge and gazing at itself in a little mirror. Love is always rather vain. But it wasn't exactly beautiful. It was pale and gaunt, restless and malformed, and its veins were knotted from years of stress. Of course it saw nothing of its own ugliness, for, as we all know, Love is also blind.

The spirit perched on the edge of the bed—this was Klingsor's chance. He grabbed the pincers and gripped it firmly by the neck. Love uttered a few squawks and dropped the mirror.

The noise woke Lancelot—always a light sleeper. In an instant he was on his feet, his hand on the sword drawn from under the pillow, and he started towards Klingsor. When he realised who was standing there he lowered the weapon, feeling at once confused and rather suspicious.

"Is that you, Klingsor?" Lancelot was sorry to have caught his host in such an embarrassing situation.

"Yes … I came in … I thought I'd see how you were sleeping."

"But why have you got those pincers in your hand?"

"Well, you know, if an insect happened to be disturbing your sleep, I could catch it."

"You'd use a thing like that to catch it? I find a sheet of paper works very well."

"I'm very squeamish by nature."

"And have you caught anything?"

"Oh, yes … but nothing important."

And he showed him the Love spirit.

"Phew, it's ugly," said Lancelot, and he lay down again, still feeling rather doubtful.

Klingsor went back to his room. He stuffed the spirit into a bottle, carefully capped it with some parchment and string and stamped it with the royal seal of Solomon. On the side he attached a little label bearing the words '*Amor, amoris*, masc.', and placed it up on a shelf with the other bottles of spirits. The Love spirit swam round and round in the liquid, like a mournful frog. Satisfied with his night's work, Klingsor went back to bed.

"If only I could do such a good deed every day," he sighed earnestly, and quickly fell asleep.

The next day Lancelot woke to something remarkable: the sun was already high in the sky. He was so astonished he simply remained where he was, not moving, for ages. For the last seven years he had woken every day at dawn and leapt out of bed in a state of frantic anxiety, and now he felt little inclination even to get up. He dressed very slowly, and gave little thought to putting his long curls in order. As for shaving, he just didn't bother.

"I look quite elegant enough for the dragon," he thought to himself.

Eventually he made his way down to breakfast. Klingsor gave him a delighted reception.

"How did you sleep? And what did you dream about?" he wanted to know.

"What? Oh, yes, that I lost my spurs in a muddy field."

"That's a pity. Because the first dream you have in an unfamiliar place usually comes true."

"That would be a shame. You know, what with the price of wheat these days, my estates aren't doing as well as they used to, and I really hate unnecessary expense."

"It might have been better if you had dreamt of the fair Queen."

The colour drained from Lancelot's face. It was true! For the last seven years he had dreamt of Guinevere every night, and now … he had even left her blessed name out of his morning prayers, for the simple reason that he had entirely forgotten to say them. And he'd been awake for a whole hour, and if the magician hadn't mentioned her he wouldn't have given her a moment's thought.

Still in a daze, he took his leave of Klingsor and set off for the road that wound up the mountain. The magician stood waving after him.

"Not happy yet," he murmured, stroking his beard. "He still hasn't noticed the blissful transformation inside him. But sure enough, in time he'll come to bless an old man's memory."

And he sobbed with emotion.

Lancelot trotted along the road for several hours, deep in thought. Then the way turned into a little beechwood.

A woman on a donkey was approaching from the opposite direction. Before her and behind, the donkey's back was piled high with fine-looking loaves. A baker's wife, evidently.

"God give you good day," he called out politely. The knight without a stain always made a point of greeting women first, including peasant women. The baker's wife returned his greeting.

The wench was not unattractive. Indeed, her plump, homely manner had a fragrance of its own, like the bread.

"Aha, you must be Amalasuntha," Lancelot began. "Didn't your late grandfather make wafers for the Bishop, and didn't you offer three candles last Easter so that you might see the Archangel Gabriel face to face?"

"No," the woman replied.

"Ah, then your name can only be Merethén. Two of your four children have died of smallpox, but the third is doing wonderfully well. There is a blue hedgehog on the sign over your shop, and you are rather partial to trout?"

"No," the woman replied.

"Right, that's enough small talk," said Lancelot. He dismounted, tied the woman's donkey to a tree and lifted her down from its back. The loaves on either side stayed where they were.

Some time later they returned to the highway. Lancelot helped her back up onto the donkey, settled her in between the loaves, untied the beast and sent it off down the road. He stood for a while waving after them in a friendly fashion, then mounted his steed and continued on his way.

But he had gone barely five hundred paces when he suddenly tugged on the horse's bit and stopped, rooted to the spot. He took out a finely embroidered kerchief and mopped his brow. It was dripping with cold sweat.

The penny had dropped.

"Everything seems to confirm," he said quietly, "that I desire other women than the divine Guinevere." He remained there for a whole hour, wondering what the explanation might be. During this time, to his horror and embarrassment, the image of the baker's wife kept rising up before his mind's eye, followed by a succession of others—a captain's widow, two grape-picking wenches, a person of ill repute, and Guinevere's three chambermaids. Only the Queen was missing.

In deep gloom he continued on his way until sunset. As night began to fall he passed through a rather charming little town with a handsome, high-roofed inn calling itself The Famous Griffin. He would gladly have stopped there for dinner, but it would have meant being late for the dragon. It usually emerged from its cave only in the early hours of darkness, to drink.

He arrived at a grim wood, where the strange shape of the trees, the dark green cliffs and fearsome airborne cries signalled the proximity of danger. He steadied the lance in his hand and, following his instinct, rode directly into the place where the air of menace seemed greatest. Only then did he begin to wonder why he had not encountered a single shepherd or ancient mountaineer warning him to proceed no further.

The way was precipitous, and, tormented by hunger, he was becoming ever more impatient. Finally he came across a great pile of human bones. At the start of the next turning he could see a cave. To the expert eye its shape betrayed, quite unmistakably, that it was tailor-made for a dragon. Bearing his lance stiffly before him (he had earlier taken care to remove the little English flag) he advanced warily.

But who could describe the rage he felt when, on reaching the entrance, he spotted a large notice announcing in flowery Gothic lettering that the dragon had since moved house, and now resided in the cave under the peak popularly known as the Dead Mountains' Carnival Doughnut.

Lancelot knew only too well that the Dead Mountains lay some twenty miles to the north, and that, moreover, with its many precipitous ranges and three infamous passes where thieves waited to plunder travellers, the route, even ignoring the poor transport arrangements of the period, was not generally considered a very agreeable one.

After much humming and hawing, he turned his horse round, went back and stopped for the night at The Famous Griffin. Dinner began with some white breast of chicken, finely sliced, followed by a large carp, a highly spiced and very tasty leg of veal, some rather unusual regional pastries and a basket of superb apples. The wine was no less satisfactory. But the greatest surprise of all was that he wasn't miserable.

Nor did his misery return the next morning. The sun shone. There was a cheerful clonking of bells under his window as a line of cattle went past on their way to the meadow, and the whole beautiful world was filled with the comforting smell of manure. The breakfast liqueur (a light vermouth) and the rabbit pâté that followed were both extremely pleasant. Lancelot felt an irresistible urge to bathe in the lake and then fall asleep in the grass.

And then he remembered the dragon, the three mountain passes bristling with robbers, and all the dismal hardships of the life of derring-do. For some hours he waged a difficult struggle with himself.

Finally, towards midday, he pulled on his boots and, thus attired, stamped his foot decisively on the floor.

"No, I won't!"

And he set off, back towards Carreol, without the Queen's shoe. And the dragon lived happily ever after, in its cave under the peak of the mountain popularly known as the Carnival Doughnut.

"He's only human, after all," Lancelot told himself.

A curious dullness crept through his brain. He was living in a new universe, one in which everything was pleasant and amiable—and that was precisely what was so terrifying and incomprehensible. The landscape of this new world was so impossible to find his way around that it simply annihilated thought. He felt like a man who has drunk a great deal of beer. And not without cause. He had knocked back a pint at every hostelry along the way.

And thus he arrived at Carreol, where Arthur held court in those days. He washed off the dust of the road and prepared to enter the exalted presence of the Queen. But he had barely stepped out of the door of his lodgings when he bumped into Gawain, who greeted him with the exciting news that it was two all at half time in the crucially important jousting tournament between Cornwall and Wales, and promptly dragged him along to watch. After the match there was a banquet in honour of the victors. Lancelot completely forgot himself in the general jollity, which continued until well after midnight, and it was only the next morning that he remembered his audience with the Queen.

By the time he reached the Palace she was already out walking with her ladies in the park. Fortunately he was very familiar with the route she took, and he dashed off to take his place behind the lime tree whence, according to the courtly custom that had grown up over the years, he would step out into her path, as if by chance, as she came strolling by.

But he arrived too late. She was already in the avenue. To hide behind a tree and then instantly reappear from behind it now seemed a rather pointless formality.

He knelt before her and kissed the hem of her garment. An ambiguous smile played on her lips, and she did not immediately pronounce her usual "Pray rise, worthy knight!" until Lancelot had grown tired of kneeling and a degree of irritation had infused itself into him.

"They tell me you came back yesterday," she suddenly remarked.

"That is so, my lady," he replied, blushing.

"Indeed? Then rise, worthy knight," she declared, but with an offhand brusqueness that reduced the time-honoured phrase to a casual insult. Lancelot was deeply disconcerted. What worried him most was that the Queen's anger seemed so distant—as if it had not been directed at him at all.

"My lady has grown even more beautiful in my absence, if that were possible," he ventured, both clumsily and without any of the old sense of his heart in his throat at the sight of Guinevere's newly enhanced beauty. She was extremely beautiful, to be sure, but some little monster hidden in the trees had whispered in Lancelot's ear: "So what?"

"From which it is quite clear that you have never loved me," she continued, somewhat illogically. "I simply do not understand your behaviour. But no matter. The question is—have you brought my shoe? Hand it over!"

"Indeed, my lady," he stuttered. "That is to say ... as regards the shoe ... I forgot ... I left it in my lodgings."

"You left it in your lodgings?" (eyebrows raised to an impossible height).

"Strictly speaking, it isn't actually in my lodgings, it's ... "

"It's where, precisely?"

"That is to say, on my way back, it was stolen from me ... "

"From you, the knight without a stain?"

"Now I remember—it was during a card game. I was forced to offer it as a pledge. To an Ishmaelite."

"And how many heads did the dragon have?" she suddenly asked.

"Just the one," he replied guiltily.

"And you didn't cut it off!" she yelled.

"No. What happened was … "

But he was not allowed to explain. The Queen looked him up and down with unspeakable disdain, then turned her head away and made off at great speed, trailing her female entourage behind her.

Lancelot stood there, his head down on his collar. He had lost the Queen's favour! He had expected the thunderbolt. He had expected the ground to open under his feet. He had been prepared for his soul to sizzle and flash as it was cleft in twain in indescribable agony. But the lightning had not struck. The ground, and his soul, had not been cleft in twain. In the new world in which he found himself, it seemed there were no thunderstorms, only little squirrels in the branches, and babbling brooks among the trees, and a general beer-swilling happiness. It was horrible.

That evening, over dinner at court, the Queen made his loss of favour clear to all by calling for Gawain to pass her the peaches. The next day the whole town was talking about it. Whenever Lancelot entered a room in the palace, the laughter instantly stopped and the ladies of the court gazed at him with tears in their eyes.

Lancelot threw himself into gambling, won steadily, bought himself three new horses and a first-class sword, and went carefully through his bailiff's accounts. He took out two books he had purchased in his youth, Cato's *Wise Sayings* and Peter Abelard's enthralling tome on the Holy Trinity that had caused such stir in its day. He resolved to make himself perfect in the Latin language. Suddenly his life had so much more scope than before. And it pained him grievously. What pained him beyond words was that he was no longer miserable.

The time came when he could deny it no longer, and could even say it out loud:

"I do not love Queen Guinevere."

The whole miracle was both ugly and incomprehensible. Such things did not happen in the course of nature. You might lose a pair of spurs, or an overcoat. You could even mislay, as he once had, a sword. But not Love! Except of course by magic. And he remembered the night he had spent at Chatelmerveil.

Lancelot was a man of action. He was instantly on his horse and speeding towards Klingsor's castle.

From his tower the magician saw him coming and hurried out to greet him.

"He's come to thank me for my kindness," he whispered, and tears welled up in his eyes.

But Lancelot leapt down from the saddle and most decisively seized the magician by the beard.

"You scoundrel!" he bellowed. "Uncle of dogs and lover of bitches! But why do I waste words? Give me back my Love this minute!"

"Oh, oh, oh," sobbed Klingsor. "So you haven't been any happier all this time? Don't you see now how much broader life is, and how full of interesting things, when you're not bound hand and foot to love?"

"Stop mouthing, you cousin of toads and hedgehogs, fiend and Devil and all his works!" Lancelot added vigorously, and gave Klingsor's beard a twist. "Give me back my Love, this minute!"

"As you wish," Klingsor replied, with a disappointed sigh.

He led Lancelot into the castle. From the row of bottles he took down the one with '*Amor, amoris*, masc.' on the label, cut the string and lifted the Love spirit out with his pincers. He wrapped it in a wafer and handed it to Lancelot, who swallowed it with a glass of water.

A few seconds later Lancelot shuddered violently. His entire body and soul were torn with pain. His knees shook, his head buzzed and the world darkened before his eyes.

"I have lost the Queen's favour!" he gasped. He clutched his throat and dashed out without so much as a word of farewell.

The pain was so intense he had difficulty staying on the horse. His tears flowed, and he lowered the crest of his helmet so that no one would notice his shame. But they flowed so copiously that they leaked out under the visor and ran down his armour.

And he was happy.

1935

MUSINGS IN THE LIBRARY

L OOKING BACK on the blissful days of my youth, as they begin to slip away from me, I can now see that the best of them were those spent in the Bibliothèque Nationale in Paris. I won't deny that the hours I whiled away on night watch at the Scouts camp were also very pleasant, and my first amorous embrace, up in the mountains of Austria, though pure puppy love, comes pretty close— love and nature have seldom let me down. But the very best moments were undoubtedly those spent in the Bibliothèque Nationale, especially the winter evenings.

Now, the beauty of penny-pinching is perhaps that it is so typically French. No illumination of any kind was permitted to penetrate the ever-receding mystery of the huge space under the arched ceiling. That would have been wanton extravagance. Instead, tall green lampshades, placed at strictly rational distances apart, burnt directly over the tables. These were of course switched on only after total blindness had set in. Immediately the silence intensified, humming with feverish excitement, since closing time was now imminent and everyone's life suddenly depended on getting through the next fifty pages. The only sound to be heard was the rhythmic, monotone rustling of pages being turned and the occasional voice raised in protest by some superannuated lunatic at the counter where the all-powerful ushers were enthroned.

At five minutes before a-quarter-to-six, a personage specially assigned to the task would proclaim in a voice of thunder: "*Mesdames et Messieurs, on va bientôt fermer*"—the closing '*er*' being wonderfully drawn-out, wavering off to vanish in the remoteness of those never-to-be visited rooms where the library kept its millions of books. Then, at five forty-five precisely, the same functionary would call out, with all the succinctness we have come to expect from ancient prophets of doom: "*On ferme!*" And everyone trooped out.

My friend Swen Reimer filed out with me. As we made our way across the vast courtyard in the gathering gloom, I spotted the girl I had been admiring on and off throughout the day whenever I needed a break from my reading. Now, as she crossed the space in front of us, there was no difficulty deducing her national origins. In her crisp trench coat, blue student's cap and powerful stride there were distinct adumbrations of the Prussian military.

"You know, Reimer," I observed. "If I were German, I'd go straight up to her and announce: 'Young lady, you are German, I am German. Shall we leave together?'"

Then something dreadful happened. Reimer replied:

"Yes, I might just do that, but I'd have to be on my own." Then, "Do excuse me," he continued, in his usual, slightly offended-sounding tone, and promptly abandoned me. He was with the girl in an instant, seemed to strike a chord with her almost at once, and the two of them marched off into some erotic hinterland, leaving me standing there as if turned to stone.

It was an unspeakable disappointment. I had always imagined that Reimer would be just as timid as all the other souls who haunt the libraries of the world. I had no sense of his being in any way superior. I had felt sure of him, I had complacently despised him, and now … That's what happens when you put your trust in people.

I wandered through the Place du Palais Royal, where I was particularly struck by a display in the window of the Louvre department store. It presented a stork bringing dazzlingly lit presents to dazzlingly lit children sitting in a little house, in which the gifts appeared in rotation and then miraculously disappeared. It reminded me that Christmas—that ritual humiliation of the selfish and the lonely—was creeping up on us. I carried on down the Rue des Saints-Pères, where I lived, thinking how pleasant it would be if there were a letter waiting for me in my room.

"Even better would be one with a cheque inside," I mused, more pragmatically. "But should some female acquaintance have written, that would at least be something. I wouldn't even mind going back to the customs office, so long as there really were something for me in the post, something completely unexpected."

Regarding the customs people: I once had to go there to register my presence while they opened a parcel that had come addressed to me from some person or persons unknown. I stood trembling before three officials while they withdrew a large cardboard box from its brown paper wrapping. They opened it, very cautiously, and discovered a thick wad of cotton wool. The suspicious wadding was then dissected with professional expertise.

Hidden in its depths was a tiny flower—an autumn crocus. The 'amusing' Gallic anecdotes that followed showed their true mentality. For my part, I smiled a superior smile and thought it ridiculous to have been summoned to the main offices for this. But at the same time I was deeply moved. For, apart from the rose and carnation, which of course everyone knows, the autumn crocus was the one flower I could identify by name. In fact I am always delighted when I see one, as for once I can be sure that it isn't a snapdragon, or salvia, but incontrovertibly an autumn crocus.

In other ways too the post stands for the element of unpredictability in my otherwise straightforward life. On one occasion I received an invitation to a ball with "I'll be there" written on it in an unknown hand. On another occasion I was sent an old-fashioned tie-pin that arrived, as I worked out later, just in time for my name day. Then a Mickey Mouse badge appeared one Christmas Eve. And once, at a time when I was asking myself with particular bitterness just why I had to live in Paris—so far from Budapest, my beloved home—to embrace the self-imposed exile in the cause of greater knowledge that afflicted a whole generation of young Hungarians between 1924 and 1930, the postman brought me a perfumed envelope containing a ticket for the Budapest transport system, already punched.

I tried not to think about who the kind sender might be. At the time I had no one in my life. I had arrived from Hungary two years earlier, having cut every tie and entanglement. All my relationships had been decisively terminated, I corresponded only with other men, and then always very briefly. For this steady stream of little surprises I impersonally gave credit to the post office itself, or ascribed it to my fate as written in the stars, and their inscrutable way of protecting me from the mortal sin of terminal loneliness.

Nor had my stars—that celestial arm of the French postal service—forgotten me on this fateful evening. In the box behind the keyhole I found a letter, addressed in a hand which needless to say I did not recognise. I opened it with palpitating heart. For the sake of brevity, I reproduce it verbatim:

Most Respected Doctor X,
I hope you will excuse my writing to you as a stranger. My cousin, whose letter is enclosed, told me that that you wouldn't mind. I arrived in Paris a few days ago, and would like to work in the Bibliothèque Nationale. I would be enormously grateful if you could advise me about what I need to know.

Respectfully yours,
Ilonka Csáth

It was accompanied by a few lines from Edit Wessely, now calling herself Mrs Gyula Somebody.

My dear Tom,
Would you please take my little cousin into your much-vaunted care. She is very pretty. Behave yourself at all times, and don't cheat on me with all those flappers.

Edit

This same Edit had been my great love at university, the heroine of endless poetical walks in the Buda hills. I had been very fond of her, but since then she had done the dirty on me and married, as had increasing numbers of my former acquaintances. As for this Ilonka Csáth, I knew nothing about her. With my usual inborn pessimism I reckoned she would quite probably be obese, and almost certainly stupid. Never mind. The main thing was that my faith in the old post office had not been disappointed. So far everything that it had brought had been propitious.

I carried on up to my little room. This 'room', like that of every other Hungarian intellectual in Paris, was the smallest, ugliest and most humble abode imaginable; and like the room of every other Hungarian intellectual in Paris, it has become so glorified in memory that it outshines all my other paradises in all their variety.

After some humming and hawing I composed the following reply:

Dear Colleague,
I would be happy to put myself at your disposal in the Bibliothèque Nationale at any time. You can identify me by the brown handkerchief I wear over my heart, and more particularly, by the fact that I always sit in seat number 266. If not there, I am to be found in the coffee house going off to the right.
Yours etc.

And gradually I forgot all about her.

Then one morning I became aware of a young girl moving hesitantly along the central passageway dividing the two sections of the library. She was behaving the way people do when checking the seat numbers in a cinema to see which is theirs. Finally she stopped next to my table, glanced at the people sitting on either side of me, blushed, took out a work of reference from the nearest bookcase and began flicking aimlessly through it. She was very pretty. All the same, I carried on reading.

It occurred to me that this could well be Ilonka Csáth. She was obviously wracking her brains trying to decide which one was me. (Young lady, I am your man. Perhaps you should speak to me. But then again, perhaps you aren't Ilonka Csáth. Women can be divided into two groups: those who are Ilonka Csáth, and those who are not. Representatives of the latter greatly outnumber the former. Oh, nonsense …) And I continued with my reading.

Once I had fully understood the next sonnet I glanced up again. The person in question was no longer there. I felt just a little put out, disappointed and betrayed. Something might have come of it. But that's women for you—they always go away. And she was so very attractive. I read another two sonnets, then stood up and set off for lunch. When I reached the door, the same very attractive young lady got up from the next table and ran over to me.

"Excuse me," she said, in appalling French, "but aren't you Tamás X?"

"I am indeed," I replied in Hungarian, "and you are most probably Ilonka Csáth."

She was delighted by my perspicacity.

"I thought it must be you, but I was afraid to say anything."

"How could a grown woman, a university student, be so shy?" I asked, in a rather superior tone. "So, in a word, you would like me to initiate you into the mysteries of the Bibliothèque Nationale. I would be delighted. But what would you say to the idea that we first have lunch?"

"Lunch? I … I usually just have coffee."

"You poor thing. So you're having to watch the pennies?"

"Not at all. But I'm not yet used to going into restaurants. This is my first time away from home, you know."

"Then you must get used to it with me. I know a very good, and cheap, little Czech restaurant, where you can get authentic Hungarian food. Real pork chops and cabbage, just like at home."

"Yes, that would be nice," she answered uncertainly.

I took her straight there, my behaviour a rather odd mixture of the paternal and the gallant.

Over the meal I asked her for news of the university. She was very chatty, endlessly informative about the ways of the teaching staff and the reaction of the students to their lectures.

She was one of those rare girls who don't come apart at the seams the moment they open their mouths. For all her shyness, she expressed herself precisely and thoughtfully, and once she warmed to her theme the sentences flowed, sweetly, lyrically, eloquently. She was a second-year arts student, just twenty—which nowadays means little more than adolescent. She was still young enough for intellectual merit to make a strong impression on her.

We got on wonderfully well. She was so much like a colleague I almost forgot that she was such an attractive young woman, and I would have loved to take her to my bosom. I even tried to pay for her meal, despite the state of my finances. But, true to Hungarian custom, she refused so adamantly it was as if I had impugned her respectability.

The afternoon passed in what seemed a moment. How proud I felt, leading her timid steps round the catalogues and the pigeon-holes where orders were placed, and explaining the inner meaning of the pictures, all as if I personally had discovered the art of printing. I taught her everything that mattered. I pointed out the more egregious old-timers, sitting there poring over their books—the old gent with his blue cap who would stand up from time to time and whistle for a few minutes; the one who never stopped munching away; the mad one, and the talkative one who had discovered the primal human language from which all others could be derived. And when we went for coffee, I declared rather fancifully:

"Don't let it worry you that ninety per cent of the people you see in here are geriatrics, cripples and lost souls. It's not only an asylum for the likes of them. It's also a refuge for the eternally young—people like you and me, for example—and in fact all human life … "

I just couldn't find logical expression for my feelings.

But in fact Ilonka was in little need of reassurance. It was obvious on that first afternoon that she would be completely at home in the library. Perhaps this was because her sensitivity and timidity found a protective calm in the ordered, reliable, studiously innocent world that is scholarship, of which the library is the outward and visible embodiment. How comforting it is to know that everything is in its place, and all so aloof and impersonal. Moods and desires come and go, like so many restless tourists, but the folios remain in place, waiting benignly to be read by succeeding centuries. Buses, taxis and metros rush us about at frantic speed; placards bawl out every grubby little change in our material lives: the library stands for what is pure and true.

At closing time I escorted her back to the students' hostel where she was staying.

"What are you doing after supper?" I asked.

"Nothing, really. I'll talk to the girls for a while, then go to bed and read."

"And the night life of Paris, doesn't that interest you? Have you been up to Montparnasse?"

"No, and I've no wish to. I don't like being with lots of other people. Besides, I couldn't go there on my own."

"Then come with me."

"I couldn't. I've only spoken to you for the first time today. After all."

Her moral sense reassured me. It told me she was a proper Hungarian girl.

"Don't you feel lonely at night? Don't you miss your mother?"

"Not today. Today I'm really happy."

I didn't understand.

"Well … there's the library. I'm so happy to be working there. And you've been so good to me. Will you help me again, some time?"

"But of course, gladly … I really don't enjoy the evenings. For me, it's the most difficult part of the day."

I could have said a great deal more on that theme, but I didn't want to become sentimental. She would have taken it as a way of pushing myself on her.

"I don't want you to be sad," she said.

We looked at one another, and were silent for some time. I'm not saying it was a deeply meaningful silence. I was listening to myself and to the muffled beatings of my soul, something not to be shared with such a young girl. For a true gentleman, loneliness is a private matter.

"Well, then," I said, and smiled. I waited for her to say something. Then I kissed her hand and left.

I had gone a few steps along the Boulevard Saint Michel, still sensing the soft touch of her hand on my lips, when I had the sudden feeling that someone was following me. I turned around, and there she stood.

"Please don't be angry. I wanted to give you this cigarette holder … you were so good to me."

I was so surprised all I could do was grin. But before I could formulate any meaningful sentence in my head, she had slipped away, swiftly and silently, on weightless steps. The cigarette holder was one of those you can pull out to a really impressive length. I was thrilled with it, but at the same time something told me I should be asking myself why a girl who spent her days in a library should have given it to me. I filed it away as a memento of the Bibliothèque Nationale. That seemed to me right and proper—due payment for scholarly services rendered. After all, I had devoted an entire afternoon to her.

After I had known her about a week, I managed to persuade her to come with me after closing time to the Rue d'Antin, to try my favourite vermouth.

There is a rather special little place in the Rue d'Antin where the only drink on offer is the Italian vermouth known as Crocefisso. The place has the sort of odd-looking door you find in English pubs—no top or bottom, just two swinging wooden boards in between to stop people looking in. This strange door seemed to create a strong impression of moral degeneracy in the girl. She recoiled from it in horror, and it took me a full quarter-of-an-hour to persuade her to go in.

The only person inside was the old *patronne*, who poured the vermouth out into a long-necked glass before each of us in turn. Ilonka spent some time gazing nervously around.

"Do you come and booze here regularly?" she asked.

"Well, if by 'boozing' you mean dropping in occasionally with one of my friends and having a few glasses together."

"I'm sure you'd much rather be here with your friends … Tell me, it really troubles my conscience, the amount of time you're spending on me."

I instantly felt an enormous tenderness towards her— the expansive, generous feeling you get when there is something you really ought to do and you actually do it.

"Truly, Ilonka, if only you knew at what a good moment you came into my life. It's made me see just how much the library, and books, and scholarship really mean to me—and that includes the bookish life itself, with all its moments of bitterness. Because now I've been able to share it with you."

She clapped her hands to her head, and her eyes took on a veiled look, as if I'd made a declaration of love. I hastened to put things right, because I believe in precision in matters of feeling.

"I think that—how can I put this?—only the selfish are beyond consolation."

"József Eötvös," she retorted.

"József Eötvös, indeed," I replied, somewhat irritably. I could not help but feel the irony of her interjection, with its unstated reproach—an irony directed at the perpetual student, with his love of quotations.

"Good," she said. "But surely I'm allowed to be grateful. Can't you see? Before I met you I didn't know which end of a book to pick up. I treated them like objets d'art. I've learnt a great deal from you."

"Please don't feel you owe me anything for that. I find it just as rewarding. It's a pleasure for me too. Taking you through those books, into my personal domain, my little empire—it was almost as delightful as initiating a virgin into the secrets of love."

She looked at me in astonishment. I had no idea where such a crude comparison could have come from, and I felt rather alarmed. But she simply nodded, and put her hand a few encouraging centimetres closer to mine on the table.

I placed mine on hers. It was very beautiful. Nature loves harmony, and the hand rarely belies the nature of the person.

However it is quite difficult to sustain a rational conversation when you are holding hands with someone. There is something intensely emotional about it, in its sheer simplicity. When a grown man takes his girl's hand he becomes a warm-hearted apprentice boy on a Sunday afternoon outing.

I felt a little more at ease when she finally withdrew hers, glanced at her watch, and said, very quietly: "Shall we go?"

She was so lost in thought she even allowed me to pay for her drink. That was the start of the catastrophe.

On the way home we scarcely spoke, and then only about the simplest things. As we were crossing the Pont des Arts, she suddenly stopped. She stood looking out over the Seine towards the Île de la Cité, and hummed the tune of a popular song to herself. I remember how much that surprised me. I would never have imagined earlier that the sort of banal sentiment you find in such a song could even enter her brain, let alone that she might hum it to herself.

That evening, as usual, I read the eternally great Casanova. Of all my friends among the deceased writers, the notorious adventurer was the one I loved most—the man who managed, in just one short life, to experience the full beauty and squalor of the most beautiful of centuries. He and I had little in common. The essential characteristic of Don Juans is that they are easy to please.

Casanova loved every woman his eyes fell upon with equal ardour, and every night of passion he spent was the best of his life. I, on the other hand, am a sort of anti-Don Juan. Women rarely please me, and then only in certain circumstances ordained by fate, when they address me in a certain tone of voice, at specially chosen moments— and even then not very much.

Strolling around the streets of Paris I simply never noticed women (and certainly none of them bothered to cast their nets out for me). I was like the man caught on film, the passer-by hurrying along the street, deep in thought, who sees nothing of what is around him and simply rushes through.

But that evening I thought of Ilonka in the somewhat disreputable light of a Casanova escapade. It had taken me a week to get to the point where she let me hold her hand … My God, how Casanova would have despised my tardiness! Because, in principle, I too was a believer in the life of danger. My heart beat in sympathy with Casanova's women and the diabolical intrigues that led to such happy endings. So why then was I so comfortably at home in mundane reality?

I shall be as cunning as old Casanova, I thought. I'll take it very slowly, one step at a time. Today she let me pay for her vermouth. Tomorrow night she's coming with me to Montparnasse … The transition from the intellectual plane to the erotic will be imperceptible. Books are the most potent aphrodisiacs, as Paolo and Francesca were well aware, and indeed—not to press the point too far— perhaps also Abelard and Héloïse.

But what would Ilonka say to all this? Without question she liked me as a wise friend, but could she accept me in another relation? Would she want to? She was so virginal, so well brought-up. Despair took hold of me once again. But I suddenly started to recall a whole series of little incidents whose significance had somehow escaped my notice: the cigarette holder ... her occasional remarks that she would always think of me whenever she read something beautiful, that sort of thing ... In fact—I realised in astonishment—she was the one who had been courting me and I, the great scholarly mind, hadn't even noticed! Oh sainted Casanova ... But now I'll show him, I thought.

The next morning I found a new Ilonka in the library. At first I thought that the alteration was in me, produced by the sudden reverse of direction in my feelings. But then I realised that the change was quite independent of my particular state. It had its own life. She was wearing a gorgeous new hat in place of the old student's cap, and she had powdered her face. The collected manhood of two tables was gazing at her in admiration—the poets, the geriatrics, even the Chinese, and her own reading seemed altogether less focused. From time to time she smiled across at me, sweetly, without inhibition.

Her change of attitude became even more obvious over lunch. The atmosphere of Paris, which seemed not to have touched her before, had now breached all her defences. She chattered away spontaneously and happily, sprinkling Parisian expressions around her sentences— I've no idea where she could have picked them up. She criticised people, found fault with the meal, and made it clear she would rather have been offered something a little more interesting. I could see that the time for Casanova-style chicanery had clearly passed, and that evening we dined on Montparnasse.

That evening, in the genuinely good restaurant, the supposedly timid Ilonka revealed a surprising assertiveness. In the Czech place she hadn't even picked up the menu. Instead, with a mixture of modesty and unworldliness, she had simply left the ordering to me. This time she scrutinised the list with great cunning, and managed to pick out a meat dish that proved totally inedible. The wine we drank was Haut Sauterne, since I had once heard that that was what you ordered if you wanted to seduce a woman. I don't know what effect it has on women, but it made me extremely witty. Ilonka, who never betrayed the slightest trace of humour, listened to all my opinions with the greatest deference.

After dinner we went into the Viking Café bar and drank cognac. We sat on a cosy leather sofa, very close together, in the Parisian manner. Reimer was sitting at one of the nearby tables with the German maiden, and we exchanged conspiratorial smiles.

"I hope you don't mind my saying this, but we're just like a loving couple," I observed.

"If it doesn't bother you, then it certainly doesn't me. My nine aunties aren't going to ambush us in here."

"Tell me, Ilonka … have you ever been in love?"

"I'm not saying. You never tell me anything."

"Me? What should I be telling you?"

"Who you've been in love with, and how much—those sort of things."

"But you're not interested in my little life."

"Not in the least. Only, I would just love to be able to hypnotise you and find out some of your secrets. I'd love to be able to read you like a book. Oh, Tamás, Tamás, you're so stupid!"

I kissed her hand, with great emphasis.

"My little girl!"

Ecstatic happiness floated down on green clouds from the ceiling above us, with its collection of suspended model boats. For the moment I was indeed in love, and I gazed in adoration at this girl who had turned the compass needle of her heart in my direction. But in that instant Casanova, in his billowing black cloak and rice-powdered wig, stepped back into my consciousness.

"Poetic feelings aren't quite enough, my young friend," he said. "There must be action, I humbly suggest. Action."

But no action followed. Instead it was Ilonka who proposed that we go for a walk.

"It's only just eleven," she added. "Let's take a look at the banks of the Seine."

"Splendid."

"But we need to remember, I have to be back at the student hostel before one. Nobody is allowed in after one. The other day a girl was made to wait outside until morning."

"Well, they're so highly moral, these French," I said. "The sort of depraved hussy who isn't back by one deserves to spend the night with her boyfriend."

I now knew what I had to do to carry out Casanova's advice. Somehow I had to fritter away the time, in ways that she wouldn't notice. If she wasn't back by one she would come and sleep with me out of sheer insecurity. The flood of ideas pouring in on me made me quite dizzy.

We boarded a taxi and told the driver to take us to the Pont Neuf. After some inner struggle I resolved to kiss her. She leant her head obediently on my shoulder, but most decisively forbade the kiss.

"We mustn't, we mustn't."

"Why ever not? What sort of silliness is this?"

"I'm a good girl. No one has ever kissed me before."

"That's no good. Sooner or later someone will have to."

"No, I don't like it. What the point of it?"

"Some people say it's very pleasant."

"Then you should go and kiss them."

We were now at the Pont Neuf. We got out and walked, arm snugly in arm, along the bank.

"What a beautiful night," she remarked. "And how beautiful Notre Dame is. And how good it is it is to be walking here with you. Oh, *mon ami, mon ami, mon ami* … Throw that cigarette away. How can you possible smoke at a time like this?"

"Let's sit down, then."

We sat on a bench on the deserted bank of the Seine. I made a fresh attempt at a kiss.

"No, no. I've already told you, no," she said irritably. "Why do you want to humiliate me? You've treated me like a true friend up to now. You've always taken me seriously and talked to me sensibly. And now you want to kiss me, as if I were just any other girl, simply because it's an evening in Paris and it's what people do."

I let her go, and pulled myself away from her, with dull grief in my heart.

"All right, Ilonka," I said. "Now I shan't kiss you until you kiss me first. And if never, well then, never. I know you only put up with my presence because I am so terribly clever and you can use me, like a work of reference. But the moment I dare to get closer to you, as one young person with another, one living being with another … *Mais passons.* Let's just talk about the sonnets of Maurice Scève and the Lyon school of poets. The whole school was very highly regarded, even more so than your old one in Budapest."

"Tamás, don't tease me."

Slowly, visibly struggling with herself, she leant over to me and kissed me. I could sense the tears running down her face.

And now there was no restraining the kisses, as they came one after the other, with a strange, lachrymose happiness, and went on until we were gasping for breath. They came from the other side of so much loneliness, such barren deserts and fields of ice, these kisses, that they simply froze me as they first arrived on the hearth. But then, slowly, slowly, they became real kisses, ever more magical, intimate and thrilling.

"How clever of you to come to Paris, Ilonka. And how thoughtful of the Good Lord to provide us with the banks of the Seine."

"Oh, *mon ami*, how I have loved you, and how lonely you looked, behind your spectacles, with your Maurice Scève. And I was silly enough to think that you had been waiting for me all along, my prince transformed into a reference book. But you're not lonely now, are you?"

No, I wasn't lonely. Here was that longed-for Other, in sweet physical proximity, as far as that is possible on an embankment bench. But I still hadn't forgotten Casanova. Just half-an-hour left, and she would be turned away from the hostel.

"At last I can tell you," she continued. "My love for you isn't something that began yesterday. I've been thinking of you for two years now."

"What? But you've only known me for ten days."

She laughed.

"Really, I should be rather cross with you. I've known you for two years. Once at Edit's—but you don't remember?"

"No. These days my memory for faces is terrible."

"It's true I was only a little girl in a school uniform at the time, horribly thin, and my hair was quite different. And you never even noticed me. All you could think about was Edit. But I never took my eyes off you all evening. And I've loved you ever since."

"Ilonka! Is this possible? That someone could have loved me for two whole years, hopelessly, across such a distance, and then suddenly they just walk into my life? This is so like Ibsen's *Master Builder* I really can't believe it. And you didn't even recognise me in the library."

"Of course I recognised you, but I was so embarrassed I was too afraid to speak. I was thinking I would just go home and never try to see you again."

"But tell me … then why didn't you say anything about this before? Why didn't you give me any hint or news of yourself, for two whole years?"

"You were in Paris, and you know what a well-brought-up girl I am. Besides, if you really want to know, I did."

"When?"

"Tell me, Tamás, did you ever get that old-fashioned tie pin I sent for your name day?"

"So that was you?"

"Yes, me. And the Mickey Mouse?"

"I did. Thank you very much. But what made you choose an autumn crocus?"

"Well, I must say, it's not very nice of you not to understand."

"The crocus?"

"Yes, exactly. It was the only thing you said to me, that time at Edit's. That all you knew about the autumn crocus was that that was what it was. So I sent you one. How could you forget such a thing?"

"Sensational. Now all you have left to explain is the bus ticket."

"Oh, yes. What happened was, one day I went for a walk, all on my own, at Huvösvölgy. I was terribly sad, and I thought about you the whole time. When I got home I felt I really had to send you something from the trip, but the only thing I had brought back was the bus ticket."

"Ilonka, I am so dreadfully ashamed of myself. And I haven't given you a thought these past two years. In fact, for the last two years I haven't thought about anyone. Even now I find it difficult to think of anyone but myself. Tell me, will I ever be able to make up for my shortcomings? I see myself as a sort of water man."

"What sort of water man?"

"The one they pulled out of the lake at Ferto. He had grown membranes between his fingers and forgotten how to speak. His name was Istók Hany."

"You don't have to say anything. And you've nothing to make up for. Those two years were wonderful for me. I was never alone, and I loved you the way adolescent girls do. And now I am almost grown up, and a university student, I can travel on my own, and I've come to Paris to be with you. I'm so glad you've been alone for these past two years, and I haven't had to chase anyone else away. Because if you had been with someone, you can't imagine the wicked schemes I would have been capable of … But Tamás, what's the matter? That's the third time you've looked at your watch. My God, I'm not late, am I?"

"Not just yet, Ilonka."

"What's the time?"

"Just enough for you to get there in a taxi. It's ten to one."

What can I say? I'm no Casanova. Perhaps if I'd been a few years younger and less broken-down, I would have taken the gamble … but principally, of course … if she hadn't confessed her feelings. But once she had? It would take more than a little bit of love and a miniscule amount of audacity. The whole thing had become too much for me.

I'm a tired, cold, sardonic, bookish sort of chap, I felt. It was no good. I just wasn't up to the occasion. Like János Arany when summoned by the maiden, I answered: "It's too late. I'm going home."

Once in the taxi we exchanged not a word, we just sat there willing the driver to get us to the hostel. That is, I did. I've no idea what she was thinking.

The next day she didn't come to the library. Only on the one after, and then she addressed me only in the polite plural. Over coffee I asked her:

"Do tell me, Ilonka. What's the matter?"

"With me? Nothing at all. I been giving a lot of thought to what you said the other day about the origins of the Provençal lyric. If Gaston Paris is right, then the line of the true Latin spirit would be unbroken. But that's far too elegant to be true … I must take a closer look at Vossler."

She left Paris soon afterwards. And nothing came of the whole affair.

1934

A DOG CALLED MADELON

Unattainable are man's desires,
A will-o'-the-wisp, unreachable,
Delusory.

MIHÁLY VÖRÖSMARTY

JÁNOS BÁTKY PhD, took care to protect himself against the greyness of everyday life. As a child he even managed on occasions to convince himself that the chocolate he was eating was in fact salami. Later, he acquired a passion for cocktails. The gin in his vermouth seemed to him to embody the mighty spirit of ancient pine forests. Adding curaçao to red wine conjured up a sixteen-year-old girl—who no doubt had long since married. Women's actual faces he forgot instantly.

"What does Jenny look like?" he was wondering, one autumn afternoon in London. The walls of the little Welsh chapel that stood before him were overrun with ivy. How wonderful it is that, in the midst of all the traffic, London churches retain that pristine air of rustic piety.

The little aphorism was quickly noted down—he was a methodical man—then his thoughts returned to Jenny. Five minutes to six. If he couldn't remember what she looked like by then it would be a disaster. True, she usually wore dark blue, but that could not be relied on as an incontrovertible truth. Doubtless there would be something unmistakably Jennyish about her, but it would be as subtle as the difference between two varieties of tea. In the end, all women were Jennys.

"Hello, is it really you?" she said on arrival.

It was a good question. "At any meeting the first requirement, and the most difficult, is to establish identity," he noted (this time in his head). Here was a completely unfamiliar woman burbling away and absolutely furious because he hadn't been in the precise place they had agreed on. He waited for her to calm down, then asked:

"Won't you come back to my place for tea?"

"Oh, no," she replied, terrified by the prospect. She always was. Then they set off to his place for tea. As they always did.

Jenny was telling him about the customers. An elderly gentleman had bought a Georgian poker, a wooden madonna and a little African carving. But he had taken so long about it! And crocodiles were still very much in demand. Oh, and there were these two young men, obviously artists, who had told her that she looked like an Italian painting. What was the name of that famous Italian painter?

"Giovinezzo Giovinezzi?" Bátky hazarded.

The same. And they had asked her to dinner. But she hadn't gone. No nice girl would.

She worked in an antique shop.

"And Lady Rothesay was back again."

"Oh, was she?" he remarked, suddenly interested. (Rothesay … splendid. Such an historic name. One of their forebears was strung up by James I, somewhere in Saint Albans … he would look it up when he got home.)

"What sort of woman is she?"

"Oh, very odd. Yes, you could certainly say that. She just comes in, points to something or other, let's say a candelabra, and takes it away."

Bátky was deep in thought.

They arrived at his flat. While Jenny was making the tea (the bit she most genuinely enjoyed in the whole relationship) he looked up the Rothesays. One had indeed been hanged. His mind's eye conjured up a Scottish loch … the traditional two greyhounds sitting at the castle entrance … the melancholy Earl (a passionate collector of ivories) tippling the night away in the curve of a bay window, secretly and alone … Her Ladyship, a secret Catholic sympathiser, admitting Jesuit priests disguised as doctors through doors concealed by wallpaper … Clouds drifting across the sky in doom-laden shapes.

Once tea was over Jenny sat passively awaiting her womanly fate. Bátky remained silent.

"Now," he was thinking, "if this Jenny were Lady Rothesay, I would say to her: 'My lady, how can you do this? How could you gamble thus with your good name, when Mrs Bird next door is forever spying on us? … And besides … how could a Rothesay, whose ancestor was hanged in such tragic circumstances, lower herself to the level of someone like me, a base commoner, a mere academic? But hark! … the Earl's bloodhounds are closing in … you must fly, my lady, fly this instant! And as she was leaving, standing in the doorway with her proud head high, he would declare: 'Oh my lady, stay, if only for a fleeting moment longer! Stay, whatever cruel Fate may bring … '"

And he threw himself at Jenny's feet. Somewhat embarrassed, she stroked his hair. She had seen it all many times before.

Then everything took its usual course.

Yet again, Jenny managed to forget some item of her clothing, and when she called back she found Bátky in a terminally bitter mood. He had been reflecting on the way his whole life had been frittered away on a procession of frightful little Jennys, when ever since boyhood he had yearned for a Lady Rothesay. History held the sort of erotic charge for him that others found in actresses' dressing rooms—a truly great passion required three or four centuries' historical background at the very least. As for Jenny … it was all just lies and onanism.

"What's the matter with you?" she asked.

"Nothing. Just don't bother coming here again. Women with scrubby red hands should stay at home. And get some of that fat off your thighs. Why don't you just disappear?"

For whole days he mooched about the eternally silent streets where he imagined the English aristocracy resided when in London. Occasionally a large delivery truck would pass through, bearing the name of some famous London firm. "That can only mean a soirée somewhere," he thought, and his pulse quickened. Once or twice he managed to exchange a few words with the wife and dependents of a doorman.

"The most striking feature of the aristocracy is their invisibility," he confided to his notebook. After further thought he added: "Blondes are generally averse to fish, but go into ecstasies when served spider crabs."

By Sunday his aristocratic solitude had begun to oppress him, and he took himself off to Regent's Park with the idea of adding one of the strolling shop girls to his repertoire of conquests. Most of the time he spent watching the squirrels. There were vast numbers of them entertaining the crowd. There were also dogs. One especially interesting black creature, not unlike a Scottish Terrier but much bigger and altogether more diabolical-looking (no doubt some newfangled breed) trotted by in front of him. It was followed by a woman, whom it was dragging along in some agitation. It seemed to be looking for something, sniffing the ground with an air of busy anxiety. Finally it paused before a sort of memorial. With all the happy excitement of a purpose about to be fulfilled it prepared to transact its real business. But some inner obstruction appeared to be frustrating the process, which threatened to become rather drawn out. The dog circled round in a series of bizarre bodily contortions that were painful to behold. A crowd of little boys watched with great interest, providing an expert running commentary. The lady turned her back on the scene in some distress.

"I'll keep an eye on him, if you like," said Bátky. "Perhaps you might go and feed the squirrels."

"Good idea," she replied, and handed him the leash.

"Excuse me," he called after her. "What's your dog's name?"

"Madelon," she replied, and strolled away.

When Bátky arrived back at his tiny flat that evening he was richer by a dog. He had lost the woman in the crowd. It occurred to him that dogs have very sure instincts, and he decided to entrust himself to her guidance. They went for a stroll on Hampstead Heath, where they paused to admire the artificial lake at the top of the hill. Madelon trotted along in happy silence. They walked for hours. It was late evening by the time they reached Golders Green, where the city proper ends. Here the dog made an abrupt turn and calmly set off back towards town. Bátky realised she had tricked him. Sacrificing the money for the next day's lunch he hailed a taxi and took her home.

It was a difficult night. She refused to eat or drink. She eyed his furniture suspiciously, then crawled into a corner and howled. Towards dawn he could stand it no longer. He went out to an all-night tearoom, laid his head on the marble table top and caught a few hours' sleep.

The sun rose next morning in the sign of the dog. Bátky went home. The animal was still alive. She lay on his bed, sleeping soundly, and looking for all the world like a lady's black shawl with a fringe. The instant she set eyes on him she growled testily. And she still wouldn't eat.

He flopped into an armchair and attempted to order his thoughts. What was to be done with her? He thought of offering her to the Kensington Museum—they had several stuffed dogs on display—but his kindly heart baulked at the idea. Perhaps he should keep her, train her, and try to make friends with her? Human will-power could sometimes bring about wonders. By degrees he reconciled himself to the notion.

"We'll get used to one another," he told himself. "I've always longed for a pet, to stop me being so lonely. It's a pity the only time she'll ever get off the bed will be to wet the marble slab by the fireplace."

Whenever the tipsy cleaning lady scolded him he just listened in silence with his head hanging down. He was well used to being misunderstood.

"No doubt, after a month or two, I'll get her to come walking with me. One fine spring afternoon we'll be strolling in Regent's Park and we'll happen to meet the lady I had her from. 'Madam,' I shall say, 'as you see, I have faithfully watched over that which you entrusted to me. Madelon has grown a little since then, it is true, and yes, she has put on a little weight, perhaps, but not enough to harm her figure. Obviously she's spent the last few months in serious intellectual company. I don't believe it's done her any harm.'"

And one thing would lead to another, we'd go and have tea, then to the cinema, who knows … ? The lady, so far as he could remember, was rather attractive and engaging, with wonderfully square shoulders … simply dressed, but in excellent taste. Obviously the wife of a young but successful tobacco merchant … her father a respectable greying functionary in a large insurance company … all living in a little house somewhere, East Ealing perhaps, in one of those streets with sixty addresses on either side of the road, all exactly the same, with more or less identical lives being led inside them. Oh, the English lower middle classes, with their five-o'clock teas, their tranquil winter evenings by the fire, the single words let drop once every half-hour, most probably about the Prince of Wales …

In the afternoon the bell rang. Bátky roused himself from his reverie about the middle classes and opened the door. There stood the lady.

"I've come for Madelon," she said simply.

"Oh … oh … and oh again!" he said, lost in contemplation of the strange workings of fate. "Do take a chair. Madelon is still alive. But how ever did you find me? London is so large … "

"It was very easy," she replied. "You gave me this book to hold yesterday, while you took care of her. There was a letter inside addressed to János Bátky, Francis Street, London … I thought that must be you. I came in the afternoon hoping to find you at home. I really must apologise … I can imagine what Madelon got up to in the night … you poor man!"

"Oh, we were just beginning to make friends," Bátky replied modestly. "I stroked her the whole night. I thought you would have done the same. I kept thinking that it was your hand touching her."

"How very kind," she said, and took off her hat.

Now for the first time Bátky noticed how handsome she was. ("I've always adored tobacconists' wives. Their hair has something of the rich gold of the finest Virginia.")

They made tea, and while she was pouring it Bátky took the opportunity to record on a slip of paper: "Love affairs usually start in either September or January."

After tea he sat at her feet and laid his head on her lap. He imagined that they were now at home, in her home, in East Ealing … family photos hanging on the wall … the grandfather with huge whiskery sideburns … Christmas carols playing on the gramophone … everything serene and unchanging, the British Empire on its mighty foundations, and Madelon playing with a kitten beside the hearth.

Her lips had the taste of home-made strawberry jam. Her movements, as she undressed, were calm and placid, as if tomorrow were another day. Her whole being radiated such complete self-assurance he quite forgot to wonder at his unexpected conquest. Apparently it was what everyone did in this country after tea. Even Jenny.

"I'll come again," she said, some time towards evening.

"I'd be delighted," he replied with conviction. "Won't you tell me your name?"

"Oh, I thought you'd recognised me. You must have seen my picture in the papers—it's there often enough. I am Lady Rothesay."

And off she went.

This parting note unsettled Bátky. He placed a high value on truthfulness in other people. He had many times broken off with a woman because she said she'd been at the dentist when she had in fact been with another man. "Why was she so ashamed to be the wife of a young but successful tobacconist? These English are incurable snobs. If I had a little house in East Ealing, and a whiskery grandfather hanging on the wall, I would never dream of denying it."

Her falsehood depressed him so much he couldn't bring himself to fall in love with her. Once more his loneliness pressed down on him like a slowly lowered ceiling. The same gloom as always darkened the London streets. A fine drizzle was falling. On Camden Hill elderly gentlemen strolled towards their eternal rest. In Kensington alone there were two million old ladies. Life was quite meaningless … Somewhere, deep inside a Scottish castle, or in some dark avenue of ancient trees, the deranged wife of an earl was putting an end to it all …

One day she appeared on his doorstep again.

Once again, they spent a very pleasant afternoon. Bátky was in an intimate and sentimental frame of mind, talking about Budapest, where the cafés spilled a warm, cosy light onto the pavement, the waiters knew exactly which paper you liked to read, and the mysterious lower orders cleared the lovely white snow overnight.

"So what is your name?" he asked her, thinking that this time she would be sincere.

"But I've already told you. I am Lady Rothesay."

Bátky became cool and detached. He could see he would never get close to this woman, and what is love without a meeting of souls?

"I'm going away tomorrow, to France. My father is a tower guard at Notre Dame."

"And when are you coming back?" she enquired.

"I'm not coming back," he replied grimly.

"As you wish," she shrugged, and made her way quickly down the stairs.

A few days later the *Sunday Pictorial* found an occasion to carry yet another picture of Lady Rothesay. It was her all right.

"Women are incomprehensible," he wrote on a slip of paper, and carefully filed it away.

1934

THE INCURABLE

Peter rarely was on his way home by train from Inverness in the Scottish Highlands, where he supported a course for students on the bagpipes, at his own expense, since everyone was complaining that with the advance of the gramophone and the radio this illustrious and ancient form of music was dying out. He had just been up for the closing ceremony and was feeling very pleased with the way things had gone. If only my bear sanctuary would do as well, he mused. Another of his great concerns was that these remarkable animals had become extinct in the British Isles, and he had made a home in the Welsh forests for some bears imported from Transylvania.

But his main worry was his number-counters. He had hired some unemployed people to count up to 7,300,000 without stopping. Two had already given up, three were still counting, but when he had left London even the best of them had only managed something like 1,250,000. Where might he have got up to since?

In the express dining car he caught sight of a familiar face. It was the writer Tom Maclean. Maclean was sitting on his own, sipping spoonfuls of mock turtle soup, gazing thoughtfully into the distance, and jotting down the occasional word on his notepad.

"May I?" Rarely asked, settling himself down beside the writer. "I'm not disturbing you?"

"You certainly are, very much so," Maclean replied with obvious delight. "Please stay and disturb me some more. It would be a real kindness."

Rarely began to feel somewhat alarmed. The thought had flashed through his mind that he might not be the most eccentric person on the train.

"Because, you see, I'm working," Maclean continued. "I'm preparing notes for a radio broadcast about my Scottish experiences. At least while I'm talking to you I won't be working. Sir, the amount I have to do is intolerable. I'm fed up with myself, absolutely fed up. I've just been to Scotland for a bit of a rest. I tell you—I was there for a month—in that time I translated a novel from the French, wrote two essays and a novella, eight sketches for the *Morning Glory*, six book reviews for the *Spectator* and ten longer articles for a forthcoming lexicon entitled *Women, Children and Dogs in the Service of Humanity*. And I've still got two radio talks waiting to be done."

"That's very interesting," said Rarely. "I always thought that writers like you lay around all day waiting for inspiration, and then wrote only once it had struck. You seem to have a lot more to do than my own rather simpler sort of millionaire."

"I've no idea how hard a millionaire works, because I heartily dislike those sort of people, present company always excepted, of course. But the number of things I have to deal with has become more than I can bear. You've just heard what my holiday consisted of. You

can imagine how much I do when I'm actually working.
I have to submit two novels to my publisher every year,
three articles for the paper every week … then there are
my book reviews and reader's reports. I have to dash off
the odd novella to show that I am still a creative writer,
plus the odd bit of scholarship, so that I don't get dulled
by all the other writing; oh, yes, and the publicity notices
for my friend's books, and the little demolition jobs on
those by my enemies … What does all that come to?"

"Monstrous. How do you manage it? When do you do
all this writing?"

"You should really be asking, when do I not? I fall asleep
writing, and wake up writing. I plan my hero's fate in my
dreams, and the moment I open my eyes the signing-off
phrase for my radio broadcast comes into my head."

"And when do you live?"

"Never. I've no time for sport, and none for love. For
years the only women I've spoken to have been the ones
bringing manuscripts, and believe me, they aren't the
most congenial. But that's not the real problem. The
problem is finding time to read."

"But you've just been telling me about your book
reviews and reader's reports … You must surely have to
read those, at least."

"Oh yes, sir, I read an appalling amount—six or seven
hours a day. But only the sort of things that publishers and
editors lumber me with, or books I need for something
I'm writing. Do you know, I would really love to read
a book purely for its own sake. Something that'd be of
no use to me whatsoever. The stories of Hans Christian

Anderson, for example. For years I've been dying to read *The Ugly Duckling* and I've never got round to it."

Rarely pondered this for a moment, then blurted out:

"But why the devil do you work so hard?"

"For a living, my dear sir, to make a living. You of course wouldn't know this, but ordinary people have to earn their crust. With you, its almost automatic. I'm not a popular writer, my books aren't suitable for turning into films, I don't have the sort of brazenness that would enable me to write plays. I'm just a grey literary journeyman, and I have to slave away morning, noon and night simply to make ends meet."

"If I might ask a rather impertinent question, how much do you earn?"

"Five or six hundred a year."

"What? For all that work? That is appalling. My heart really goes out to you. And you aren't even a dying art-form, like the bagpipes."

"I will be, sooner or later. Nobody wants the sort of thing I do."

"Listen here, Maclean. I've a proposition to make. I'll pay you a thousand pounds a year. Now, don't jump up in excitement. Of course I'm not giving it to you for nothing. In return I would ask you, as from today, not to write another word. Not a single one. Do you accept my offer?"

"Do I accept? What a question! Do you think if my guardian angel flew in through the window I'd give her a good kicking? Sir, you are restoring me to life and humanity. There will be tears in my eyes every time I pronounce your name. Sir … my angel … henceforth I shall spend all my time fishing. And chasing women, women who don't bring me manuscripts, and who never open a book. Illiterates, in fact. And I shall read *The Ugly Duckling* and the *Summa* of Thomas Aquinas. And I shall be the first happy writer in the history of literature. Because I won't be writing."

A month later Tom Maclean was visiting his sister Jeannie, the wife of Colonel Prescot, who lived in Bournemouth. They were talking over lunch about their far-flung family—uncle Arthur the country doctor, and his wife who wore such very odd hats; Alastair, the famous seal hunter; John, who had bought a farm in South Africa and sent native penny whistles to the children; Mary, who had just married again, and poor Charles, who would never amount to anything.

"And how are you, Tom? Tell me about yourself," said Jeannie. Since their mother's death she had played a somewhat maternal role in his life. "Are you working a lot?"

"I'm not doing anything these days. I haven't written a word for a month. I go fishing, and I read the foreign papers. I've learnt Portuguese—a wonderful language. Now I've come home for a week's walking. I've bought myself two puppies—Sealyhams—and I'm training them up. And as for women … " And he lapsed into a bashful silence.

"Splendid. And are you happy?"

"Happy? I'm only now starting to feel really myself. I used to be a slave. The last dirty slave. These days I live like the Good Lord himself. In France."

"I'm so glad, Tom, really glad. Because I've been wanting to say to you for some time that you should relax and join in with things a bit more. But what I don't understand is why you look so unwell. You face is rather pale and careworn. Why is that?"

"I've no idea. Perhaps all the walking—"

"It's as if you're not really satisfied, Tom. Look, I know your face. There's something missing in your life."

"No, no. You're quite wrong about that. I've never felt so well. I feel like a god!" he shouted angrily.

Jeannie was so astonished she made no reply.

They took coffee in the sitting room. Then Tom went through to the family library to stretch out and do some reading. There he found his fifteen-year-old nephew Fred sitting at the desk, scratching his head.

"Hello, Freddie. Why such a miserable face? Is something wrong?"

"Wrong? It's this pesky homework! I've got this essay to write for tomorrow, about Shakespeare and Milton. I'm supposed to 'compare and contrast' them. Isn't that crazy? Why were these two blighters ever born? And it's Bournemouth v Aston Villa this afternoon."

"Shakespeare and Milton? Hmm. You know what, my lad? You go off to the match, and I'll write your essay. It'd be a shame to waste such a fine Sunday afternoon. Shakespeare and Milton. What a joke!"

"Would you really, Uncle Tom? I always said you were a thoroughly decent chap, Dad can say what he likes … "

And out he dashed.

Two hours later Jeannie came into the library. She found Tom working away feverishly, surrounded by densely scribbled sheets of paper, with a Shakespeare on the floor and Milton and the other classics scattered everywhere. The moment she entered Tom glanced up at the ceiling to show his irritation. He clearly didn't take kindly to being interrupted.

"What are you doing, Tom?"

"Oh, er … I'm helping Freddie with his homework. 'Compare Shakespeare and Milton', I ask you! At first glance, you'd never think what a good subject it is. I've written fifteen sides and still hardly touched on the matter. I think the teacher will be pleased."

A few days later Tom Maclean called on Peter Rarely. He found the millionaire in his music room, working on an experiment to get thirty parrots to speak in chorus. He nodded briefly as Tom entered. The parrots, who were in the middle of *God Save the King*, fell silent.

"Sir," Maclean began, very formally and clearly embarrassed. "I am compelled to renege on our agreement. I must ask you not to remit the usual sum next month. I'm terribly sorry. I know it's not exactly playing the game, but I really have no choice in the matter."

"What? You want to start writing again?"

"Again? Now I want to start in earnest. So far I've just been lazing around. I've got the outlines of a five-volume novel sequence, an autobiography of indeterminate length and a life of James IV of Scotland. It's time I really got going on them."

"But haven't you been happy without your writing?"

"No, sir. It's just no good. If you threw me in prison I'd write in blood on my underwear, like that Mr Kazinczy my Hungarian friend told me about. I wish you good day."

1937

FIN DE SIÈCLE

THE CHESHIRE CHEESE PUB in London is famous for having remained exactly as it was when the great Dr Johnson, that commanding figure of eighteenth-century English literature, sat there and delivered his immortal banalities, so faithfully recorded for posterity by the assiduous Boswell. The most distinguished poets of the age have met there ever since—towards the end of the last century, for example, it was here that Tyrconnel, Lionel Johnson, Ernest Dowson and John Davidson held their weekly reunions.

On this particular occasion only three of the quartet were present, Tyrconnel, Dowson and Johnson. Tyr–connel was holding forth. He was a languorous, deeply unconventional Irish poet, as signified by the single curl of silky black hair that strayed so casually over his forehead. Hardly a week went by without his having made some new mystical discovery, some fresh instance of telepathy, perhaps, or some interesting notes he had come across inserted by an archangel into a piece of Old Irish prose. He chatted away about such things with the easy familiarity and volubility with which others might discuss a football match. This was in marked contrast to Lionel Johnson, who would deliver his observations about the weather in the manner of a revelation: "There was a thick fog in Chelsea this morning," he would regularly announce, and glare balefully around the room, his hand clapped on some invisible sword.

"You deal out a pack of cards marked with mystical symbols," Tyrconnel was saying. "The important thing is the square grid on the back of the card. It gives you the matrix in which the secret meaning is contained. Then, if an adept studies the cards at a particular hour of the night, his visions will correspond directly with the symbols. If the card stands for Public Esteem, he will be looking at his future career. If he draws the symbol for Heaven, he will learn the nature of the greatest happiness that lies in store for him … "

"Very interesting," observed Lionel Johnson, with his customary decisiveness.

Tyrconnel's face reddened slightly.

"I wouldn't be telling you all this, Johnson, if I hadn't seen some extremely convincing experiments carried out in our little group."

"In our little group" was a regular saying of his, though it was never quite clear in what species of secret institution or laboratory these improbable researches were conducted. Johnson and Dowson never asked. They were afraid that he might already have told them, only they hadn't been listening at the time.

After this, Johnson spoke about his new *Tractatus*, in which he would show once and for all that Bloody Mary had been quite right to send the Protestant martyrs to the stake. Tyrconnel listened with great interest. He did not for a moment believe in Johnson's Catholicism, any more than Johnson did in his mystical anecdotes. He knew that it was all part of the business of being a poet, the licensed eccentricity of the poet's view of the world. The precise nature of the world view didn't matter—what did was the burdensome honour of the vocation, in which verse forms amounted to dogma and symbols represented political affiliations.

Then came that memorable business with the Scots.

Davidson, the one Scottish member of the group, finally arrived. Without a word of forewarning he had brought along two of his fellow Scots—tall, thin, badly dressed young men with grey, baldly staring eyes. They sat themselves down with an air of embittered arrogance, the way Scots often do, and proceeded without the slightest inhibition to pour scorn on Tyrconnel's mystical revelations. This did not particularly bother Tyrconnel—he was not a man who took himself seriously—but then one of the newcomers suddenly barked at Lionel Johnson:

"And why aren't you drinking?"

"I never do," Johnson replied coldly. "You know, when I was still quite young I once fell on my head … "

But his interlocutor was not going to let him digress. He made his contempt for Johnson's asceticism abundantly clear. He poured scorn on everything he considered unhealthy, decadent, over-refined and self-consciously crafted. In his opinion only the Scottish peasantry were worth anything in this world, and no serious writer could get by without drawing on the ancient, undiluted wisdom of the Gaelic people and the primordial power of the ballad tradition.

The three lyric poets listened to this for some time, with polite smiles on their faces, much as Saint Sebastian had done on a similar occasion. They stroked and played with the dog under the table, then suddenly stood up and took their leave.

All three knew, without a word being said, that it was the end of their weekly reunions for ever. They could never again return to the Cheshire Cheese without exposing themselves to the risk of a further meeting with the two Scottish representatives of the Primal Force. They themselves were gentlemen of far greater refinement, *fin de siècle* to the core and Englishmen to boot, and they could think of absolutely nowhere else they might meet, that is to say, without asking Davidson to dispense with his Highland friends. Thus these convivial gatherings, of such great significance in the history of English literature, came to an end.

Having escorted Johnson home, Tyrconnel remained out in the fog, sensing the utter emptiness of his life. As he drifted from gas lamp to gas lamp a strange feeling gnawed away at him—the same sort of half-conscious preoccupation you get when a particularly attractive woman steps onto the train while you're chatting to your friends—you hardly notice her, and no one quite realises why you all keep turning your heads in one direction, until eventually you spot her. But this particular concern, when he finally identified what it was, was not quite so appealing.

"What would happen," he asked himself, numb with horror, "if Johnson really were serious about his Catholicism? Might that also mean that those two Scotsmen genuinely believe in their Life Force? Then I'm the only one … the only one … "

But he allowed the absurd idea to drop. His thoughts turned, rather more consolingly, to Dowson, the love poet of transcendent delicacy who, in real life, spent his time playing cards with the father of his beloved—a greengrocer—and chatting away, no doubt, in the lowest form of cockney. Such is human nature.

Thus he arrived at a certain nightclub. Here, behind the sleeping back of the early-retiring Victoria, the nocturnal decadence of a highly moral age seethed and bubbled away like a virulent organism in a sealed bottle. Tyrconnel was well known in the place, not as a mystical poet but as the son of his eminent father, who sent him large remittances every month. His personal decadence found partial expression in telling dirty stories to the Alhambra chorus girls, who pulled their chairs into a ring around him because they enjoyed them so much. But this simply intensified his inner emptiness, and he drank steadily to fill the void, if only physically.

Some time later he was joined by his countryman and fellow poet Oscar Wilde—devastatingly elegant, as always, in his tail-coat, and languidly witty as ever. He had just come from some place or other where he had been the life and soul of the party … but what frightfully hard work it was, keeping up his non-stop brilliance! With the audacity of an ageing voluptuary, and one eye on his audience, he set his hands to work on the chorus girls, all the while murmuring in Tyrconnel's ear about his one great grief, his unrequited passion for a certain young earl, a blond to boot, to whom he penned sonnets of classical perfection the way Shakespeare once had. How mendacious are the ways of poets! Tyrconnel knew all about the seedy-looking stable boys and hotel flunkeys who hung around outside Wilde's house, draining off his rapidly diminishing funds. That was the real truth about poor Oscar.

A wave of alcoholic grief swept over him. He leant his head on Wilde's shoulder and murmured through his tears:

"Babylon and Nineveh … "

Wilde stared at him in astonishment.

"For God's sake, not you too, old chap? You're not starting on this religious nonsense too? They tell me our dear Lionel—"

"I've come to realise," Tyrconnel explained tremulously, "that I'm just as beastly a humbug as you, and those two … sons of the peasantry, with … with their Primal Force … and Lionel Johnson … who's never had proper dealings with a woman in his life … But I … I happen to know a real human being … an itinerant tinker … drowned at sea off Inverary … "

And he launched into the story of the tinker, knowing full well that, as with everything else in his life, there wasn't a grain of truth in any of it.

"I lie only when I speak, you lie even when you don't—that is the difference between us," Wilde declared aphoristically, and got up to go and repeat the witticism at several other tables.

Tyrconnel made his way home, taking one of the chorus girls with him, and paying her about as much attention as he would to a bus ticket.

Tyrconnel sat in the presence of the Great Publisher, having politely placed his newly purchased grey top hat on the floor beside him, and his snow-white gloves and ebony walking stick with the onyx handle on top of it.

"I've been thinking about a weekly journal," the Great Publisher announced, "the sort of thing they do in America, something a lady might hold in her hand on the train. The cost would be recovered through advertisements for spas, watering places, that sort of thing. But of course that side of it wouldn't interest you, as a poet. Naturally, the paper would mostly carry puzzles, photographs of the Royal Family and stories about dogs. But I also want it to print sonnets and Platonic dialogues—in a word, literature."

"Indeed," Tyrconnel murmured respectfully.

"But not the sort of 'literature' you get in *John o' London's Weekly* and suchlike. Mine will carry only the best, the most refined writing of the day. Nothing but Symbolism and that French stuff that no one understands. Which is why I thought of you, Mr Tyrconnel. You will be in charge of the literary column. Your fellow workers you will naturally choose yourself."

Tyrconnel immediately thought of Lionel Johnson and Dowson. It was now a full month since he had seen them, and he had begun to miss them almost sincerely. It was not so much a case of the heart going out in friendship— that sort of thing was out of the question between them— rather, he missed the permanent but always stimulating sense of oppression that he felt in their company. What kept them together was a feeling of mutual fear. Tyrconnel was filled with pangs of genuine remorse every time he thought of Johnson's immense Oxford-educatedness and the stubborn asceticism with which he worked, rewriting and polishing his verses until they were either absolutely perfect or consigned to the bin. He himself wrote swiftly and haphazardly, and then a kind of hysteria amounting almost to panic, or the simple fact that his cigarette had gone out, would be enough to stop him taking any sort of corrective action.

Dowson was different again. He would produce no more than four or five poems a year, but it was precisely this indolence that the prolific Tyrconnel felt as a perpetual reproach. The man who writes very little always has the advantage over the one who writes a lot, since his every phrase is carefully constructed; just as the person who stays silent is always cleverer and wiser than the one speaking.

Naturally, Tyrconnel did not know the actual address of either of his friends. He had often accompanied Johnson home, but had never noticed the name of the street, let alone the number. In truth, the only things he did notice were either written or spoken: just words.

The one positive thing he did know about was the gossip he so regularly repeated, both in his editorial capacity and at literary dinners—that Ernest Dowson spent every evening from eight onwards in a certain little pub the far side of London Bridge, playing cards with his beloved's father, a greengrocer. Had Tyrconnel been English it would undoubtedly have restrained him from intruding on the hidden other half of his friend's life. But his Irish soul was tormented by a mischievous delight in causing embarrassment. That evening he roused himself and set off in the direction of London Bridge.

He quickly identified the little pub from its coat of arms. He went in, knocked back an Irish whiskey at the bar (he was a great patriot) and enquired after Dowson. Not a name anyone could recall. But when he wrote it out in large simple letters, and explained that the person regularly played cards with a gentleman who owned a greengrocer's shop, the barmaid's face lit up.

"Oh, you must be thinking of Mr Ernest." And she took him into a back room.

In the thick haze beneath a paraffin lamp several people sat at cards. It took him some time to spot Dawson's aristocratic profile. By then his friend had already noticed him. He jumped up, came over, and shook his hand vigorously. He was deeply embarrassed.

"Hello, old chap. This really is kind of you ... excessively kind ... I'll introduce you to my partners, if you like, but, please" (pulling him closer and whispering), "you won't let on, will you, that ... you know ... I sometimes write verse. That sort of thing puts a chap in a rather difficult position here."

There were three people at the table: Mr Higgins the greengrocer, his shop assistant, and his daughter.

"My friend Mr Smith," declared Dowson, and blushed furiously. "Mr Smith is in bicycles."

His connection with the newfangled sport bestowed a certain prestige, and Tyrconnel improvised a couple of highly interesting stories about the problems of the cycle trade, gazing all the while at the girl with friendly admiration.

He was thinking of the Trojan elders—the moment they set eyes on the Fair Helen they knew that the war was justified. Yes, Dowson was absolutely right. It was perfectly logical that a man who counted recent admirals and foreign secretaries among his long line of forebears should revert, in matters of taste, to the earth from which he had sprung.

This Miss Higgins was your typical English country lass, with bulging muscles, the ripe bloom of an apricot on her cheeks and the stereotypical blonde hair that is the especial pride of the Anglo-Saxon race. Her glance was as amiably expressionless as the face of one of the larger domestic animals, and nothing Tyrconnel said was met by the least glimmer of understanding or produced the slightest spark of interest.

They rose soon afterwards, and left. As they crossed London Bridge Tyrconnel filled his friend in on his future plans. The idea of a weekly magazine delighted Dowson, and he promised to be extremely diligent and write a poem for every second number, or at least every third. Moreover, he knew Johnson's address. They piled into a two-wheeled cab and set off, with the coachman's white top hat lighting up the London night from the dizzy heights of his seat behind them.

They found Johnson at home. He was sitting at his desk, in his dressing gown. Its subtle resemblance to a monk's cowl was tactfully offset by its sheer elegance, as if to deprecate any such suggestion.

"I'm sorry I can't offer you port or cigars, but I don't keep that sort of thing in the house. But I came by an excellent Devonshire cider the other day."

The cider was decidedly of the first rank. Johnson did not have any himself. He seemed rather to look on it with disdain.

Meanwhile Tyrconnel was explaining his plans to him, this time in rather more colourful terms. They were standing on the threshold of a new literary movement. The time had come to bring the Symbolist cause to public attention, and only they, the Esotericists, could do this.

Johnson listened with an expression of profound understanding. When Tyrconnel finished, he placed his hands together on his chest and began an even longer exposition.

"My young friends," he declared—*inter* a great many *alia*—"you always concern yourself with the mere Form. But the problem is, what is really important? Naturally

I am not thinking here of the fashionable problems of the day—housing conditions in the slums, the origin of species, the still-unclear role of woman and other such trumped-up issues. What we need is a return to the time-honoured questions. Our real concern in the journal must be that great conundrum, never yet properly addressed in the West, the Conflict of Universals. We must give a fresh hearing to the Realists, who established that general propositions do exist in reality, and equally to the Nominalists who regard them as just so many words, *flatus vocis*—pure wind—as they so delicately put it. We must pave the way for a New Scholasticism."

There was much more in this vein. It got deeper and cleverer as he went on. But by now his two companions were utterly lost. They had not the slightest idea what to think about Abelard, or why the conclusions of Saint Thomas Aquinas were so definitive, or where the otherwise so immensely gifted Duns Scotus had gone astray, or indeed why the system proposed by Grosseteste was untenable in the light of the fiendishly clever attacks on his thinking by William of Ockham.

Johnson rose, and took a few steps towards the doorway.

"And then, of course, there's Saint Anselm of Canterbury … "

At that precise moment he collapsed and lay stretched out motionless on the floor.

Filled with unspeakable terror, Tyrconnel and Dowson dashed over to him. As they leant over him, they caught a strong whiff of brandy. He was completely drunk.

The Kabbalistic cards lay in the drawer of the writing desk, each in its individual leather case. Tyrconnel had been given them by his friend Russell, who wrote under the pseudonym A E. He was considered a leading expert on all things occult, and his crystal-clear verses remain splendidly impenetrable to this day. But Tyrconnel left the cards where they were. He didn't even glance at them. He had come to regard his mysticism as no more than the sort of passing phase in his development he should put behind him, now that he had discovered his true self. Even so, to ensure that the time he had spent on it had not been wasted—though a dreamer he was also extremely ambitious—he composed a deeply symbolic narrative poem for the journal about the hardships faced by an Irish sea monster called Manannán. The only bit really dear to his heart was the creature's name—Manannán.

A day or two later there was a knock at his door. It was the famous seer and mystic Mary Spottiswoode, one of the glories of Russell's little circle. And there she was, fluttering down the vestibule as if on wings, with the air of someone about to swoon. She looked particularly winsome that morning, with her feathered hat, enormous boa and parasol.

"She looks like some kind of bird," Tyrconnel thought to himself (no doubt with a goose in mind).

"The cards," she whispered. Her face was interestingly pale, with the desolate world-weariness of someone who is forever losing things.

"Let me get you some water," Tyrconnel suggested.

"Do you still have those cards?"

"Of course I do."

"Quick, quick … "

And she sank into the depths of an armchair.

"Which one?"

"Give me the fifteenth, now, quickly. The one with the Greek letter Tau and the picture of a little bull … I mislaid it … it went missing from my pack, I've no idea how."

"What do you need it for?" he asked. He knitted his brow earnestly, in keeping with the occasion. But he had no idea what any of this was about.

"Oh," the Mystic Goose replied, blushing deeply. "How can I explain? It's not important, really. I just wanted a word with my late husband, about his will. There's a question about some of his bank deposits."

"Mary, you're not telling me the truth," Tyrconnel hazarded.

"How do you know? But why do I ask? You know everything. All the same … don't be too sure of yourself."

"My dear Mary, once a person such as myself has ascended to the lunar plane, he takes no further interest in the vanities of the world … a calm and comforting melancholy fills his soul, and a profound sense of love." (If only I knew what this is all about! he thought.)

"I knew you wouldn't take advantage of my situation. I'm a poor, defenceless woman. That is why I came to you. But tell me … last night, from thirteen minutes past one onwards … were you perhaps looking at the card with the Tau and the little bull?"

"I was, indeed," he exclaimed. (One way or another, he just possibly might have been.)

"And … oh, my God … what did you see?"

"What did I see?" A host of possibilities raced through his brain: a swan, an apple tree, a lighthouse … But then a rather different inspiration came to him.

"Oh, Mary," he murmured, taking care to choke briefly. "What did I see, Mary? It was you, you … "

"I knew it!" the Mystic Goose spluttered. The curve of her neck was lovely and white. "And I saw you!—the whole night long. The workings of Fate … "

And she burst into tears.

"Don't cry, Mary. We would struggle against this in vain. At any rate, perhaps you should take off your hat. A swan sang in my soul all night, a wild swan from the reed beds of Coole, pure white … and how white your face is … do take off that boa … there we are. And I watched them, chasing each another across the face of the moon, with a ceaseless rhythmic motion, back and forth, back and forth—the lines of fate. How lovely your hand is! There are moments in life that rise up before us like a beacon of light in an ocean of mystery. Permit me to unbutton your blouse, Mary. You weren't wearing one last night."

"What was I wearing?"

"It was a sort of magical, pendulous dewlap, it was like … like … a shirt … and the clouds were flying beneath the moon, till I no longer knew whether it was the clouds that were moving or the moon itself … but don't be afraid of me, Mary. There's nothing wrong in this …

somewhere out there, on the cosmic mountain tops, our souls have cast aside every veil and are yielding to their mutual caresses … forgive me … I just need your girdle … yes, that's it … someone who can foretell the future … oo! oh! … the unspeakable sadness before the moment of possession … oh, you! … but sometimes the stars bring us unimaginable happiness … and then one has no right … no … no right to hold out … against the future … just abandon yourself to the waves of destiny … here, Mary, beside me … on the bearskin … yes … yes … yes … "

A few weeks later he met Lionel Johnson again, for the last time. It was just after the arrest of Oscar Wilde—not on account of the stable boys and hotel flunkeys but, more surprisingly, at the instigation of the blond young aristocrat's father. Public opinion in England, as always on these occasions, had taken a united stand against their former favourite, and people who dared take his side in pubs were beaten senseless.

At this point Johnson called on Tyrconnel, bringing Dowson with him. Dowson was even more hypersensitive and silent than usual. Johnson declared grandiloquently that they simply had to do something for Oscar. To decide what that might be, they took themselves off to a small but well-known restaurant.

Tyrconnel ordered a white Bordeaux and poured a glass for everyone. Johnson knocked his back in one go, and promptly poured himself another …

"Well, it no longer matters, now," he sighed. But he did not explain his remark.

For as long as the meal and the wine bore them up, one great plan for Wilde's rescue followed another.

"We'll produce a pamphlet in which we set out the merits of his writing, under twelve separate points, and have it signed by all the leading writers in England and France," Tyrconnel suggested.

"I think, on the contrary, we should approach the Queen and propose that she offer Oscar her protection— she has such a motherly heart," said Dowson. They also thought of enlisting the Prince of Wales' support, urging the Irish representatives in Parliament to protest, and inciting the colonial regiments to mutiny. Lionel Johnson rather fancied the idea of shooting old Lord Douglas, who had brought the case. After all, Saint Thomas Aquinas considered assassination permissible in the case of tyrants, and indeed the Jesuit Mariana made it a requirement if the tyrant happened to be a Protestant.

But when dinner was over, the coffee drunk, and they had moved on to the cognac, certain misgivings, and a mood of dejection, took hold. They began to feel like kings in exile—as does anyone who has drunk a great deal of brandy—and the futility of it all became apparent. The stark vision rose up before them of an uncomprehending age, the base multitude, and the obtuse moralising tendency of the British public. In their misery they consumed ever more cognac. Lionel Johnson seemed to cope with this surprisingly well.

Wilde's fate slowly faded before their own unspoken sorrows.

"Poor Oscar," said Tyrconnel. "But properly speaking, he was never a really good poet. His work was always too highly polished, too wilfully classical and brilliant. He never understood the importance of what is left unsaid. Never quite attained the elegant pointlessness of true art."

"The reason for that," affirmed Dowson, "was his unfortunate upbringing. I hear that the best families in Dublin would have nothing to do with the Wildes. Oscar was equally a parvenu among words. He liked to caress them the way the nouveau riche like running their fingers through their money."

"And the Church has condemned his crime even more strongly than the civil authorities," Johnson added. "If he does end up in prison, it'll give him the opportunity to repent his sins and start his life afresh."

As night and the cognac weighed ever more heavily down upon them, they began to give increasing vent to their own long-suppressed personal grievances. Tyrconnel was the first. It was easier for him, not being English. He described his desperate, sometimes feverish struggles for self-expression, the battle to liberate his work from the merely prosaic. He told them how bleak his life really was, behind the free-flowing phrases; how there were times when he could think of nothing serious to say at all; and how, in point of fact, whatever he knew about love was simply taken from books. He had become deeply embittered, and found the whole struggle hopeless. (At that stage he had no idea that he would in time become a world-famous poet, and be awarded the Nobel Prize in his old age.)

"Oh, poetry," said Dowson. "That's not the problem. I'm like a tree torn up by the roots, or some such thing."

It transpired that Miss Higgins had been unfaithful to him. The trouble began when the girl was suddenly and incomprehensibly seized with literary ambition. She poured out religious and patriotic verses, and ballads about the great English seafarers. Dowson, being so very discreet by nature, had never quite managed to reveal that he was a man of letters. Somehow he had also kept it hidden that his father was an Admiral of the Fleet and that his ancestors had fought against the Armada. He had always declared, rather evasively, that he worked in the flax and hemp business and was expecting a rise in salary "very soon". Gradually the girl came more and more to despise him as an ignorant, common sort of man. The end result was that she ran off with the deputy chief sports reporter of a provincial newspaper. "The soul is what matters," she declared. "I could never love the sort of man who is interested only in flax and hemp."

"Oh, love," said Johnson, with a dismissive wave of the hand, "and oh! to everything else in this world, and that includes all your great and sanctified ideas. In the final analysis there is only one true reality, and that is poverty."

"Between ourselves, what do you know about poverty?" Tyrconnel asked irritably.

"A great deal more than you think. All this time I've been living on my capital. I've never invested a penny in anything, because I'm not a man of business. And anyway, the medieval Church expressly condemned investment for profit," he went on, placing his hands together on his chest. "Catholicism has lost a great deal of its lustre since it quietly condoned usury. Anyway, I've always funded my spending from my capital, and this is the precise moment when it finally runs out. I shall pay the bill for my meal, and after that I shan't have a penny in the world. At the very most, the honoraria for my poems, but we'd better not talk about that."

"And what will you do?"

"I've no idea. I'll give it some thought tonight. But in point of fact, it isn't just my capital that's finished. The game's up with me too. I've already done everything I wanted to do, and had to do. I shall never write anything better than I already have. I won't, because it can't be done. I've come to the end of what is possible in the English language. I've written poetry as fine as Shakespeare's and Keats's. But I don't want to brag about that, because it doesn't amount to very much. The limits to human expression are in the end very narrow. I can't progress any further, and I'm afraid of falling back. The only logical solution would be suicide. But the Church prohibits nothing so strongly as self-slaughter," he said, and once again placed his hands together on his chest.

After the restaurant closed they spent the remainder of the evening in Tyrconnel's lodgings. Dowson lay on the rug in front of the fireplace, Tyrconnel sprawled across the divan, and Johnson sat at the writing table. The more he drank, the more monkish his appearance and manner became. The facial features of the other two seemed to blur—his had grown sharper, as in death.

Tyrconnel turned off the light and they sat like damned souls in the eerie flickering light of a tall candle, deep into the night. They all had the feeling that something was coming to an end, something truly sublime, now beyond all helping.

"Only they are happy," murmured Tyrconnel, "who, like Cuchulain, come across the Invisible People dancing in the moonlight and lie entranced in a clearing in a great wood, somewhere far, far away … "

"With the help of a little opium, perhaps," Dowson interjected.

"Most probably. Even I think that now," Tyrconnel replied. "I used to think I had no need for such chemical and scientific aids to free my soul from time and place. For example, I have those Kabbalistic cards … "

"Tell me, Tyrconnel," Johnson suddenly asked. "Have you ever actually tried them?"

Tyrconnel replied rather shamefacedly that he hadn't.

"Then why don't we try them now?" Johnson returned, rising to his feet. There was a strange excitement in his voice. "I know the Church rigorously condemns the use of magic, but it does to some extent condone the Christian Kabbalah—because it can't be used to conjure up the devil, or those evil spirits who bring mortal souls into danger. So where are these cards, then?"

With some hesitation Tyrconnel drew them from the leather cases in which they had been silently skulking.

"So, what do you do with them?" asked Dowson, as in a dream.

"Everyone picks a card, takes it home and studies it. The diagram or symbol shown on it will inspire a vision that holds the hidden solution … at least, according to George Russell. I won't presume to guarantee that this will happen. But if we really are going to put it to the test, let's each take the same symbol. Then, according to Russell, we should all see the same vision. Tomorrow we can report back to one another, or we could all three of us work our revelations up into separate poems. It'd be interesting to see how they differed."

"To hell with the individual differences," said Johnson. "Give us the cards, and let's be off. It'll put an end to this very long night."

"Look, here are four identical cards, for example, all number eights, with a full moon, signifying Love. Here are three with the symbol for Marriage. And three with the Death symbol. Which one shall we choose?"

"Why not Love?" said Dowson.

"Why not Death?" said Johnson. "It's the one most in fashion these days."

Johnson and Dowson went home, each with a card in a leather case in his pocket.

After they had gone, Tyrconnel stayed up. His level of fatigue and inebriation had reached the point where a man no longer feels tired and for a while his brain remains clear and sober. He aired the room, tidied it up, then leafed through a Dublin periodical. From time to time he heaved a great sigh. Life, he felt, was utterly incomprehensible.

He decided he really should get to bed. As he was taking off his coat he came upon the leather card case, whose existence he had completely forgotten. It bore the number nine, and a Hebrew letter whose name he did not know. "Obviously the letter for Death," he thought.

"Should I really look at it?" he wondered. "I suppose I have to, since we all three said we would." In that instant he realised that it was something more than mere indifference that had made him leave it where it was. Some other feeling was at work in him, a kind of fear … Perhaps, after all …

Wanting to defer the moment, he started to cut the pages of the French novel he intended to read in bed the next morning. He was barely halfway through when he suddenly received what was effectively an order—that he look at the card. He leapt up and dashed across to the candle.

He took the card out of its leather case. At first his short-sighted eyes could make out nothing but the lines that made up the matrix. Then he noticed that they were starting to draw the face of a man. He leant closer, and dropped it in horror. It was the face of Lionel Johnson.

"Well, I did drink a fair amount," he thought. "How on earth could Johnson's face get onto the card?"

He picked it up again.

Once again his friend's image appeared before him. But now it was not as he had seen it earlier. It had definitely changed. The features had become much sharper. Sinister shadows were forming beneath the eyes, and the jaw seemed to have sunk a little, as if all the strength had gone out of it.

He threw on his coat and hat and dashed out into the street. Luckily a cab was waiting at the corner. He shook the driver awake and gave him Johnson's address.

Arriving, he leapt out of the cab. At that precise moment a second cab stopped at the door, and out jumped Ernest Dowson.

"You too?" Tyrconnel asked, with a frisson of horror.

Dowson nodded in affirmation. They raced up the four steps and began to hammer on the door. No response. They pummelled and kicked it, in a rising frenzy of impatience and hysteria.

The commotion produced a policeman from some-where. Normally the streets of this well-to-do neigh-bourhood were completely deserted.

"And what are you up to, then?"

"We've come to see Mr Johnson."

"Mr Johnson came home earlier, perhaps half-an-hour ago. If he wanted to let you gentlemen in he would already have done so. He clearly does not wish to see you. You'd better go home."

"My God, you must help us get this door open somehow."

"What makes you say that?"

"Something terrible has happened in there … "

The policeman considered this.

"His doorman went away this morning. Mr Johnson is there on his own. Hm … Right, let's go."

He fetched a crowbar and prised the door open.

They found Lionel Johnson in his bedroom. He was lying on the bed, in his dressing gown, which now looked even more like a cowl. His facial features had become much sharper, and the lower jaw had sunk slightly, as if all the strength had gone out of it. His heart had stopped.

Brain haemorrhage, the doctor decided.

1934

THE DUKE

An Imaginary Portrait

ANYONE whose meanderings around Italy have led him to the little town of Cortemiglia, in the Alban hills near Rome, will have been sure to look over the palazzo, the one feature of note in the place apart from the famous paintings in the cathedral that so greatly resemble those to be seen in the cathedrals of every other little Italian city. Indeed the Palazzo Sant'Agnese itself is hardly different from the thousands of other fine Renaissance and Baroque examples across the land. But if you do ever find yourself there, take a closer look, and you will be struck by the mellow, formally correct beauty of the place, and the magical sense of the past that lingers broodingly over it.

Indeed the building has now arrived at precisely the state most appropriate for such musings—for the past, for history itself, to reach out to you as a living reality. Here there is no glittering spectacle such as you find at Assisi, cleaned and tidied up for the tourist; nor is it so stark in its abandonment as to convey a feeling of oppression, of exhaling the miasma of the ruin of centuries. Virginia creeper clambers the walls at will, with a sort of spontaneous Italian artistry. Grass grows unobtrusively between the paving slabs in the grand courtyard, but nowhere runs to wild profusion. The palazzo is maintained and open to the public, though it takes a full half-hour, with the help of the ever-obliging and undemanding local street urchins, to rouse the custodian from wherever he might be and procure his services.

Once the outside of the building has been properly admired, the interior does not disappoint. Everything inside the rooms is of the finest materials, crafted in the most aristocratic taste—that is to say, nothing produced in our time comes anywhere near it. From the windows of the upper floors a serene, dreamlike view opens out towards the haze of blue sunlight on the distant Tyrrhenian Sea. On one of the windows some poetical Englishman, or perhaps Englishwoman, has used a diamond ring to engrave Keats's well-known line—*A thing of beauty is a joy for ever.*

And like the refrain of a poem, two motifs confront you at every turn. The first is the family coat of arms, depicting two swords and an ostrich feather. The second is the face of the man who commissioned it, Marcantonio Sant'Agnese. The Duke's portrait, with its prominent nose and meaty cheeks, and their suggestion of opulence, not to say ostentation, is by Rusticaia. The full-length painting, in which he poses before a half-drawn purple-brown curtain, is by Marzio Filiboni. Behind the curtain can be glimpsed a wide, blue-green Renaissance landscape, with rivers and lakes, and tiny, toy-sized mountains. With his brow wreathed in laurel and a purple cloak draped over his ceremonial armour, the Duke stands foursquare. He is magnificently obese. His obesity is even more striking in the equestrian statue, by Mastagli, that stands in pride of place on the main terrace in the ancient park. Next to it is a fountain, on whose rim sits a nymph holding a little elephant in her hand. The water tumbles out though the elephant's trunk onto an assortment of tritons, who struggle to hold their spiral conches up beneath its downpour—or rather, would struggle, if the water were ever to flow from the spring again. The fountain is later than the statue, executed in the manner of Bernini in the middle of the seventeenth century. Naturally neither the full-length portrait nor the statue gives any clue to the Duke's psychology, but seeing the portrait one can imagine that behind those two tiny and not very benevolent-looking eyes, between the self-confident and grandiose meatiness of the corpulent cheeks, lurks a strange sense of panic. And the viewer might perhaps wonder what sort of person Marcantonio Sant'Agnese could have been in real life—in his long-ago life, in that long-vanished time.

The origin of the Sant'Agnese family was derived by Renaissance scholars from Agnosos, one of the heroes of *The Odyssey*, who is known only from a synopsis of the great cyclical epic. It records that this Agnosos was rescued from the waves by Pallas Athene's owl when the Four Winds were misguidedly let out of their bag and promptly capsized the Greek ships. By happy chance the bird brought him to Italy, where he founded the family line with the help of a mountain nymph. More reliable chronicles assert that the original forebear was a Lombard hero called Balmungo, who took an active part in the assassination of King Alboïn and was rewarded with extensive domains in the vicinity of Benevent. Other accounts propose descent from Saint Agnes herself, but considering the saint's well-known virginity this argument runs into certain difficulties. Whatever the truth might be, the fact is that at no time in the sixteenth century did the family play a role of any significance in Italian history, until one of its scions, as Callixtus VII, attained the throne of Saint Peter. Thereafter his brothers and cousins became bishops, papal generals, treasurers, *gonfalonieri* (governors of the more distant Christian lands) and lords of various lesser dukedoms. The Pope's one grievance was that in all his long and illustrious reign he never managed to acquire an independent little principality for his own family. Nonetheless the Sant'Agnese wealth grew in this period to such legendary proportions that it rivalled those other nepotistical dynasties the Borghese, the Barberini and the Pamfili.

Marcantonio Sant'Agnese, who was born in 1561, stepped easily into the possession of wealth, grand titles and princely self-confidence. Of his infancy and youth nothing is known, from which we can infer that he went through all the formative childhood experiences that scholars of the period would consider typical, though none left any discernible mark on his character. As a young nobleman he is known to have played a role both at the papal court and in the diplomatic machinations of the Roman aristocracy, and to have taken part in intrigues prior to papal elections. He forged a treaty with the Duke of Modena, negotiated an alliance with the Viceroy of Naples, took money from the wife of the

Catholic Spanish King for working against the rather
more Christian-like King of France, and from the King
of France for working against the King of Spain …
In a word, he was active in all the usual historical and
political manoeuvrings of his time.

Such political dealings were conducted in this period
partly through protracted and highly secret negotiations,
including offers of bribes, and partly by the staging
of grand parades and other public spectacles. From
detailed contemporary reports we know, for example,
that Marcantonio was involved in the procession of
unparalleled brilliance arranged in honour of Hassan Bey,
the Christian convert half-brother of the Prince of Tunis.
Three liveried retainers bearing the huge family coat of
arms led the way. Next, robed as Neptune and riding on
a camel, was a herald holding aloft an embroidered silk
banner depicting the martyrdom of Saint Agnes. Then
came two soldiers, dressed as Moors in chains, followed
by two knights in armour. These last carried a banner
stretched out between them, printed with the words of a
sonnet proclaiming that once the heathens had murdered
Saint Agnes, but now they came to worship her—the
point being that Hassan Bey had been received into the
Church in Sant'Agnese dei Tre Torri, by none other than
Matteo Sant'Agnese, the bishop-uncle of our hero.

There followed twenty noble members of the ducal
court, on horseback, with lances at the ready, each lance
bedecked with a little olive-green flag, and the heads of
the horses and knights all resplendent with huge ostrich
feathers. Next came the Duke himself, dressed from head

to toe in olive-green brocade, as was his horse, down to
its hoofs, with the famed Sant'Agnese jewels, fabulous
emeralds, visible below the feathers on its head. Apart
from the ring and the legendary clasp pinning the three
olive-green ostrich feathers of such fantastic size to his
cap, the Duke never wore jewellery himself. This was
to signify his *contemptus mundi*, a fashion newly imported
from Spain. His own horse and those of the courtiers in
the line ahead had reinforcements of pure gold attached
over the usual iron shoes, loosely, so that most of them
would drop off during the procession, to the delight and
advantage of the Roman populace.

In the footsteps of the Duke trundled a huge theatre-
cart of the sort that you can still see in the carnival at Nice
today. Drawn by four fully dressed horses, it represented
the temple of the goddess Bellona, Marcantonio being a
strong believer in military glory. In front of this classical-
style temple rose a pyramid composed variously of lances,
cannonballs and the decapitated heads of Turks. Behind it
stood four women in immense hooped skirts embroidered
with olive-green quivers, and wearing gold-embroidered
headdresses. These were Bellona's attendants. The age
could not imagine any ladies of stature, whether human
or divine, without (even in their more intimate moments)
an accompanying flock of attendants.

Inside the temple, the Goddess herself, in the person
of Imperia Ottomini, sat enthroned. She was robed
alla antica, that is to say, rather scantily, to display her
splendidly ample curves. Ladies at this time were much
taken to dressing up as classical deities, reasoning that

as such they could afford greater pleasure to onlookers than would be possible in contemporary costume, which covered the person completely, apart from the face, and revealed nothing of the beauty of the female form. Hence Imperia Ottomini, enthroned as the Goddess of War. But neither she nor the Duke wished to present too grim or uniformly martial an aspect, and what emerged from her quiver was not arrows but little artefacts made of sugar, which she held out to a child and a tiny Maltese terrier standing in front of her. The banner above this scene proclaimed: *The blessings of warfare*.

Love played a large part in the life of Marcantonio Sant' Agnese, that is to say, the love he bore to Imperia Ottomini. No doubt there were other liaisons too, but about those history is silent—in contrast to some fairly lively accounts of his relations with Imperia, which certainly did leave their mark in the pages of historical scholarship.

Imperia was the wife of a nobleman called Guiliano Ottomini. This Ottomini was a member of the Duke's innermost circle. He made frequent journeys as his diplomatic representative, and in time became the chief overseer of all his domains. From which it clearly follows that he was not in the least troubled by his wife's intimate relations with his employer, and no doubt took the same gentlemanly and accommodating line with her children, all of whom carried the Duke's blood in their veins. Which makes it all the more surprising that in 1589 the Duke had this useful and extremely tolerant man murdered. This event is recorded in many sources, consistent in every important detail.

One night Ottomini, who was in Rome, was visited by a messenger on horseback, sent by Marcantonio to summon him urgently to Cortemiglia. The nobleman jumped on his steed and set off at once. A few streets down the road, near the ill-lit Teatro Flavio, six desperadoes who had been lurking behind a corner leapt out in front of him, fired their pistols at him, then repeatedly stabbed him as he lay wounded. The papal police rushed to the sound of the shooting, and raced off after the killers. Three of them managed to take refuge in the palazzo of the Spanish legation, where they could not be pursued any further, since it enjoyed diplomatic immunity. But three were caught, among them the popular mountain bandit Luca Perotti, who was generally known to be in Sant'Agnese's pay. The papal court sentenced the three men to death and, once it became clear that Sant'Agnese would make no objection, carried out the executions. A huge crowd followed Perotti on his last journey, and listened with deep emotion as he confessed his sins on the scaffold, in splendid verses, which he sang.

The reasons for this murder can be only surmised, and then very tentatively. There might possibly have been serious disagreements between the Duke and his steward over the accounts, as Konrad Schneyssen argues in his mighty tome *Einführung zur Geschichte der päpstlichen Nefen* (*An Introduction to the History of Papal Nepotism*), but that seems rather unlikely, since all the signs are that up to the very moment of his tragic death Ottomini enjoyed his master's complete confidence and continued to carry out important assignments on his behalf. It is also difficult to imagine that after so many years he, for his part, would suddenly begin to disapprove of his wife's conduct. We ourselves—though, in the total absence of hard fact, this is mere conjecture based on the way people thought at the time—would hazard the view that the murder of the unfortunate Ottomini was another example of Marcantonio's gallantry towards Imperia, a sacrificial offering made by her lover. There is no doubt that Imperia was a very demanding lady, and the Duke did not stint in offering testimony of his passion, showering the woman he loved with jewels, estates, sonnets penned by his own fair hand and portraits of her; and when he could think of no other way to offer even greater witness of his adoration, he had her husband murdered, as proof for her and the whole world of the unquenchable and boundless force of his passion. The fair Imperia seems to have accepted this extreme manifestation of his love, for not long afterwards she finally moved into the Duke's palazzo, and remained his loyal companion to the end of his days.

The murder of Ottomini seems to have produced a major spiritual convulsion in Marcantonio. His Court Chaplain, the Jesuit father Marcuffini, who was renowned for the great saintliness of his life, took the view that the only road to absolution lay in the sanctity of repentance, and insisted that he should now give Imperia up for ever, on the grounds that the nature of his 'regrettable error' meant that to persist in the relationship would expose his soul to continuing mortal danger. Marcantonio, as a deeply religious man, would no doubt have readily undertaken any humiliating act of penance, especially one of the more picturesque and public varieties favoured by the age, but he had no intention of leaving Imperia: time makes every man the slave of custom. His spiritual crisis lasted almost half-a-year. During that time he lost a great deal of weight and incurred vast expense for the constant attendance of his doctor. Quite how the crisis was resolved is not clear, but what is beyond doubt is that at the end of that half-year he took part in a large-scale religious ceremony in Saint Peter's, which seems to confirm that by then he had indeed undergone the 'sanctity of repentance'.

In his aforementioned work Konrad Schneyssen offers a rather different account of this episode, but we should bear in mind that, as a Protestant, his purpose is to use every weapon at his disposal to place the Church in a bad light. More recent historians have cast considerable doubt on his conclusions. For example, Aldo Lampruzzi, that outstanding representative of the sceptical spirit prevailing at the end of the last century, questions whether Sant'Agnese was implicated in the murder at all. He considers it simply a matter of contemporary gossip, unsupported by any documentary evidence or demonstrable fact. In more recent years, that elegant Neo-Catholic and Royalist French historian François de Kermaniac, in his celebrated *Les Taureaux et les aveugles* (*The Bulls and the Blind*), puts an entirely new complexion on the whole affair.

He begins by endorsing Lampruzzi's argument that Sant'Agnese could not have known that the hired assassins intended to kill Ottomini. Next, the witty Frenchman continues, even if he had, he had no means of stopping them, since it is common knowledge that these brigands cared not a fig for those set in authority over them. But—and this is his most interesting contribution—even if we do think the worst and conclude that Sant'Agnese did have him murdered, we still have no right to affect moral outrage and judge his action in terms of our own altruistic, post-humanist, neo-puritanical, hypocritical and effeminate standards. The age in which Sant'Agnese— the blessed, divinely chosen Sant'Agnese—lived was the great heroic age of Europe, that is to say of the Latin part thereof, when great passions brought about equally great works and deeds, faith threw up cathedrals, Catholic solidarity raised armies against heathen and heretic alike, and love, that finest flower of the heroic spirit, swept aside all pettifogging, petty-bourgeois inhibitions (then unknown) and every other obstacle in the way, like a cleansing storm washing away so many squalid little hovels—or in this case, the smarmy little Ottomini, this "purblind, jumped-up buffoon".

While we would not wish to endorse de Kermaniac's somewhat one-sided enthusiasm, we too think it beyond doubt that there was a certain heroism, or at least an element of yearning after it, in Sant'Agnese, and that in the insatiable and sometimes almost grotesque forms this yearning took he was a true child of the age. Through the good offices of the Academy of Rome his surviving poems and letters have recently appeared in print. Among them we find plans for an epic poem the intention of which, judging from the tiny fragment in our possession, was to immortalise the military achievements of his Sant'Agnese forebears, though only a short mythological section was ever completed. In it, his ancestor Bradmart pays a visit to Venus on an Atlantic island. To commemorate the splendid night they have together she presents him with a magic root with the power to dispel even the most painful toothache within minutes.

Among the letters we find one addressed to Zsigmond Báthory, the Prince of Transylvania. In it he writes, among other things: "because you should know, my most illustrious cousin, that since our youth we have nursed no more ardent desire—in these days when Christianity itself is in such danger on its far-eastern boundaries—than to embark on a journey through the Great Wood [he means Transylvania] to wage war on the evil forces of the heathen Crescent, and so seek both atonement for our sins and the reward of the Life Eternal. How happy are you, the people of Transylvania, living so close to that famous theatre of noble warfare, in which you can take part as if on an almost everyday excursion, while we lie separated by so many thousands of miles from that longed-for arena, and our own daily excursions lead us only deeper into that labyrinth, the despised and empty life of the court, where there is nothing but misery and heartache."

In the same letter he vows that, come the spring, he too, a latter-day Dux Mercurius, will raise an army and dash to the aid of the man who has for so long inspired him to resoluteness of purpose. However, from letters written some time later it appears that previously unforeseen obstacles have arisen—first the death of a "child very dear to him" (one of Imperia's), then bouts of almost chronic toothache (it seems the legacy of the magic root of Venus had not survived for later generations) and, above all, the ongoing conflict with his neighbour—all combining to spare him that journey of "many thousands of miles" in quest of military glory.

A long-standing source of annoyance to the Duke was the little fortress of San Felice. Located just a mile or two from Cortemiglia, it represented the domain of his old adversaries, the Dukes of Porta. For years he had tried everything in his power, by purchase or litigation, to acquire it. But the Porta family clung stubbornly to what was theirs, refusing to give way even to papal intervention. Having persuaded himself that by opposing the Holy Father's will they had fallen into the sin of heresy, Marcantonio decided to destroy them by force of arms. For this purpose he bought three new cannon—so-called 'battle serpents'—and, to supplement the force already at his command, hired the notorious Mascolo band, who had plagued the borders of the Papal state for years. The bandits, who must have numbered around one hundred and fifty, arrived with a mass of weaponry, sporting huge caps, with their extraordinarily long hair tucked into hairnets. Marcantonio had them all fitted out in olive-green uniforms, and gave Mascolo the title of Commissioner-in-Chief for Cortemiglia. Preparations for the expedition proceeded at an extremely gentle pace. Before turning his mind to this hazardous undertaking, the far-sighted Mascolo saw to the needs of his own family. He packed his wife and younger children off to Naples, sent his eldest son to university in Bologna, and married off his daughter to one of the Duke's secretaries––all, naturally, at Marcantonio's expense. The bandits spent the entire winter in Cortemiglia, and the spirited independence of their behaviour caused much concern to the Duke and the townspeople alike.

Finally spring arrived, and Commissioner-in-Chief Mascolo set off with his army. He succeeded in crossing the river Nurio without hindrance, and his advance party reported back gleefully that they had penetrated into Porta territory and met with no opposition. A few days later, Mascolo's second-in-command appeared in Cortemiglia, with his regular escort of ten men, to announce the first victory in person. The troops had come across four bandits in enemy pay helping themselves to some poultry in a village. With great skill Mascolo managed to encircle all four and compel them to surrender. His men took over the village and thoroughly looted it. During the course of the night hostile forces, in an attempt to free the captives, approached with nearly thirty men to a position near Mascolo's camp. But the ever-vigilant Mascolo was on his guard, and furthermore his troops had not gone to bed that night as they were celebrating their annexation of the village. Observing this, the enemy took to their heels without so much as drawing their swords.

On receiving news of this success Marcantonio hurried off to Rome to order the suit of ceremonial armour and cloak in which he would soon be triumphantly processing into the fortress of San Felice; nor did he lose any time in securing the services of his uncle the bishop to celebrate the Te Deum in honour of his victory over the heretics. But when he arrived back in Cortemiglia there was gloomy news. It appeared that on the following day Mascolo's troops, confident of success, had advanced onto the plain that lay in front of the fortress. But there a surprise awaited them. The main gates immediately swung open and the opposing army appeared, almost two hundred men, in full armour, with trumpets blaring and extremely warlike demeanour. At this point a detachment of Sant'Agnese's force, disaffected with Mascolo on account of his allegedly unfair distribution of the first day's booty, immediately crossed over to the other side, while the rest took to their heels, not stopping until they reached their usual bolt holes up in the hills. Mascolo himself—the only casualty of the battle—was run through from behind.

However we consider this episode, it does little to suggest that Marcantonio's passionate thirst for glory had continued to grow, which in turn serves only to make him a somewhat more sympathetic figure in the eyes of posterity. We must of course bear in mind that, in the final analysis, and in terms of the great intellectual and religious achievements of the age, of its heroism and extreme fervour, Marcantonio's contribution is limited to the level of mere aspiration—rather like his little army at the fortress of San Felice. As far as posterity is concerned, the only thing of importance in the whole of this man's career may well be the one that to him would have been of the very least consequence: that in the last years of his life he formed a connection with Galileo, assisted him financially, and at the height of his persecution remained one of his genuinely loyal supporters.

As is apparent from his correspondence, Marcantonio had read Galileo's *Dialogue Concerning the Two Principal World Systems* in early manuscript form. In this work the great scientist, following the practice of the time, sets out his defence of the Copernican scheme against the prevailing doctrine of Aristotle in literary form. Sant'Agnese would surely have enjoyed the absurdities put in the mouth of one of the speakers in this dialogue, a man called Simplicius—a device that was used by Galileo's enemies to persuade the Pope that he was the intended target of the mockery. Urban VIII turned his implacable rage on Galileo, despite efforts by his supporters, among them Sant'Agnese and his uncle the bishop, to mediate between them. Galileo's now well-known fate was not to be averted, and he was forced to recant his teachings in the cell of the Holy Inquisition.

At about this time Sant'Agnese's mind was much exercised by the fundamentally new world order that Copernicus and Giordano Bruno had proposed in opposition to the system sanctified by tradition. Although not especially intelligent, through having the time and the right sort of independent mind he was able to foresee the vast possibilities that lay in their discoveries. His initial response to the new vistas opening up to a person of reason and understanding was one of naïve and almost triumphant glee, and it was only later, after he had become a convert to the new way of thinking and it was too late to shed his convictions, that he fully understood the danger.

Marcantonio's letters written in his final period give us a partial glimpse into the spiritual crisis precipitated, almost certainly, as a result of these experiences. On several occasions he grieves for the lost happiness of his youth, when he still believed that the Earth was the centre of the universe and that the sun went round it, along with the moon and the eternal stars. But now he knew that our world was just one among the countless millions, and indeed, seen in that perspective, by no means the largest or the most important, and might even turn out to be an utterly tenth-rate little star, an anonymous and quite insignificant nonentity in the mind-numbing hierarchy of heavenly bodies. And if that were indeed the case, he asks in one of his letters, with a mixture of awe and alarm, then how could it possibly be that God should have sacrificed his Only Begotten Son to redeem the same little tenth-rate star? But then, as if recoiling from the very thought, he immediately begins writing about some marvellous sauce that his new chef has discovered in the French ambassador's kitchen.

By this stage in his life Marcantonio was hardly an old man, but his tone in the letters becomes increasingly sombre. You feel there is something constantly preying on his mind. If one had to hazard a guess as to what that might have been, perhaps it would be this troubling thought—that if the Earth does not command pride of place among the stars, then what do our worldly hierarchies amount to? Once you realise that the Earth is not an aristocrat among celestial bodies, does that not imply that we can no longer truly believe in our own aristocracy? In the age of Bragmart and his illustrious Sant'Agnese forebears it would never have occurred to anyone to doubt the sovereignty of the Earth …

Marcantonio was also plagued by material concerns. He was reduced to pawning some of the family emeralds. His health was not good, and he was tortured by stomach pains. He complained that his heart was sometimes so heavy he felt he was "piling Pelion upon Ossa". His obesity at this time reached gargantuan proportions. Eating had increasingly become his sole source of consolation, and it proved responsible for his death. On 8th September 1622, against the express instructions of his doctor, he finished off a meal consisting of thirty courses, and died the following evening.

Taking all in all, it would be going too far to assert that Marcantonio played a significant role in the history of his time and country. When you consider the powerful resources at his command, it points rather to the painful ineffectiveness evident in his having lived such a profoundly unproductive life, always falling so short of his great ideals. And when we consider the truly wicked things he did—those we know of—and reflect that he probably committed many others of which we know nothing, we may well feel inclined to condemn not only the man but also the age, and the social order, that could place every opportunity for greatness in the hands of such a mediocrity.

And yet we should not rush to condemn him. Let us not forget the palazzo at Cortemiglia, with its noble elegance and aristocratic melancholy. If Marcantonio Sant'Agnese had accomplished great and famous deeds they would have vanished without trace in the passage of time, just as his moments of wickedness have passed into oblivion or uncertainty. But the palazzo remains, that exquisite object on whose windows a fine-souled Englishman has scored his sense of eternal beauty. And, taking this idea further, we may well have to conclude that it was the man's very love of pomp, his insatiable thirst for glory, his passion for that woman, and possibly even his wrongdoings and his physical grossness—and a thousand other deeply repulsive attributes that belong not so much to him as to the age he lived in—the nepotism, the anarchy, the hundred different kinds of decadence that was Italy—that made it possible for him to construct such a building. The golden iridescence of beauty is often distilled from the slime on murky water, and that is why we love the great and troubled river that is history.

1943

PART TWO

THE TOWER OF SOLITUDE

Novellas
1922–3

THE WHITE MAGUS

I N THE DAYS OF THE BYZANTINE EMPIRE in which our tale is set, many stories were told of the Princess Zoë. The only daughter of Emperor Constantine the Great, her beauty and goodness were renowned throughout Christendom, and people came from the far ends of the land to catch a glimpse of her, in her long dress that trailed stiffly behind her, on her way to church, where she would bow deeply before disappearing behind the great portal. The poor who turned to her always found her compassionate, and when she raised her slender hands in prayer some invisible blessing seemed to flow into her. It was said she could even heal the sick.

One day Princess Zoë boarded a sailing ship and spent the day at sea. It was spring, the sea was as blue as the sky, the sky was as deep as the sea, and where they met soft breezes caressed the fledgling waves. The Princess stood singing in the prow of the ship, her hair flying free. "How beautiful life is," she exclaimed, "and how young I am!"

When she returned, towards evening, the whole city was out on the seafront waving to welcome her back. The shopkeepers stood outside their shops, women crowded in windows and mothers held their children aloft. "Welcome back, Princess Zoë," they shouted. "God has brought you home safely from the kingdom of salt!" For the heart of the stone city, even as it cooled, beat inside her too, and in her face shone the classical beauty of ancient Greece, in its final and most haunting form.

When she reached the Palace news was brought to her that a little girl, the dearest to her of all her little friends, had died while she had been at sea. The cause was a long-standing but totally mysterious condition. The Princess was filled with self-reproach. Somehow she thought that had she remained by the side of her beloved little friend she might have kept her alive. From then on some inexplicable influence took possession of her. The happiness of her days darkened and gave way to the tearful melancholy of deep compassion.

The next day a throng of women came to her complaining that their children too were sick. The symptoms of the illness were always the same. The children became very cold and inexpressibly sad; they were full of longing, but for what could never be established because by this stage they could no longer speak. They did not cry, nor would they eat. Their little bodies grew steadily colder, while their faces took on a startling beauty, and by the time they died they had come to resemble the old statues of gods that householders in those days still sometimes found in their cellars. People were almost certain that through death the children were finding a way back to the happier, sun-blest lands of ancient Hellas. The doctors could find no cure, and ransacked their Galens in vain to find a name for this strange affliction.

The calamity that had struck Byzantium weighed heavily on Princess Zoë. She loved its children above everything. She felt truly at home among them and personally knew almost every child in the city. As the strange epidemic spread she busied herself night and day, going from house to house visiting the sick, comforting them and helping out wherever she could. The moment she drew near, the patient's condition would take a turn for the better. At the touch of her hand a warmer life would flow into them. They were able to laugh again, and they joined her in chanting little rhymes. When she came and sat on their beds, those who had difficulty sleeping enjoyed happy dreams, filled with wonderful and inexplicable images of the past.

But Zoë was just one person, and the sick children were many. Moreover, the moment she left the condition would return. As soon as the child was alone again, the chill took an even firmer hold. The streets of Byzantium filled with long, slow processions of tiny blue coffins.

Zoë was indefatigable, loyally accompanying every grieving mother on these last journeys. But not one of those distraught parents knew the depth of pain that she did. With every child that went to the grave, part of her own life was being buried. It was not just the mothers' tears that burnt into her heart. It was also the nameless, mysterious grief that had claimed the children, and her earnest desire to understand the fatal secret in their eyes, as they slowly faded into death.

One evening she was making her way home with her ladies-in-waiting, ostensibly to take some nourishment herself, though really she was more concerned about the fact that her women, tired as they were, had refused to leave her on her own. Along the way they called in on yet another sick little child, when she suddenly remembered that an especially dear little one, who lived at the other end of the city, was due to enter the critical phase of his illness that day. She persuaded her women to carry on without her, then she borrowed a simple, ordinary dress from the sick child's mother, not wanting the citizens to see her in the street without her attendants. If news of that reached the ears of the Court they would be punished for her misdemeanour.

She hurried through the town, almost running, but even so she arrived late. At first the parents failed to recognise her. They asked her, rather rudely, who she thought she was and why she was bothering them so late at night, and told her to mind her own business. It took some time to persuade them that she was indeed Princess Zoë, and that they should let her in to see the dead child. She placed a flower in the little boy's clenched hand and bade him a silent farewell.

Slowly, wearily, she made her way back towards the Palace. Suddenly she felt her face starting to burn, and the chilling words of farewell she had so often heard took on a fresh meaning for her, as a peculiar sensation of coldness such as she had never felt before took hold. In the dark and unfamiliar streets the wind seemed to blow with an even greater sharpness, and she glanced around apprehensively. This was a new Byzantium. She noticed, for the very first time, that everything was made of stone. The houses and public fountains were of stone, the streets were paved with stone. Wherever she went, stone temples and stone archways weighed down over her head, and the footsteps of people hurrying home clattered and rang in the street. Every one of them was a complete stranger, and the weary, indifferent glances falling on her seemed to come from an immense distance, dressed as she was in someone else's clothes, covered by a headscarf and not in the least beautiful. Zoë had only ever seen these people when they lined the streets through which her carriage was passing. On those occasions there seemed a sort of glow on their faces, some lingering glimmer of an antique radiance, and she had thought that they too were children, children who had simply grown older. But now she saw that this was not true, that on their pallid brows they carried the mark of the stone city, and it was only their constant motion that made them seem alive. She tried to fill her mind with thoughts of the sea, and the huge blossoms in the vast imperial gardens, and then it struck her that in all the windows of the city there was not a single flower to be seen—nor could there possibly be. She saw that flowers never could grow in this place— the cold withered them in the root, just as it blighted her dear ones, the children—and that she herself was the last, lonely blossom, the forgotten relic of a long-dead summer.

The road home was very long, and when she finally arrived at the Palace to find that yet more women had come to beg for a visit, she was filled with such a stupor of weariness that she sent them away without even a word of comfort. Though longing for sleep, she was so tired she could barely undress.

Her bed was icy cold, the blanket immensely heavy. Its folds seemed to have been sculpted from solid marble. Her limbs felt no less heavy, and sleep claimed her instantly.

The next morning another throng of grieving women were there waiting for her to awaken. She attempted to rise but, held down by the weight of the blanket, her frozen limbs refused to budge. She tried to explain that she was very tired, she would not get up that day but the day after—but the words simply circled round in her head, malevolently, in some strange foreign tongue, and she could not utter them. She folded her hands over her breast and simply waited for night to come.

Thus she remained for several days. Everyone who saw her during that time was astonished by how much more beautiful she had become. She was now so beautiful that it no longer gave rise to feelings of pleasure but rather of fear and horror, as at some supernatural visitation.

And they knew that she too had been struck down by the same mysterious disease that had carried off the children of the town.

The Palace was plunged into mourning. The Emperor Constantine began to neglect his duties of state. Prayers for the young Princess were said in every church in the city. Doctors came and doctors went, but there was no known cure for this condition. With the death of each child something of Zoë's own life had gone to the grave.

And then—after Thessalian prophetesses had read the signs and pronounced in vain; hermits had come out of the deserts to make the sign of the cross, to no avail; long-bearded Jews had hung up strange stones to work their influence for her, without result; Arab holy men had danced ululating beneath her window, to no effect; madmen and dwarves had turned cartwheels, and made no difference; two-headed animals bred specifically to brighten faces such as hers, had all failed—for her mysterious affliction simply grew ever deeper, more silent, more death-like—someone finally thought of the White Magus.

The White Magus had not been seen for seventy years. He lived alone, up in the north, at the top of a high mountain in the Carpathians. Since then he had renounced everything to do with the world and devoted his life to studying the eternal verities. It was said that he knew all the deepest secrets of nature and of human life. He, if anyone, would surely be able to help the little Princess.

A delegation was quickly drawn up, with the Archilogothetos at its head, with instructions to seek out the White Magus, if he were still alive, up in the Carpathian mountains.

The emissaries had to battle against many obstacles on the way. Melting snow had washed away the roads that ran between the peaks; the Danube was in flood, and crossing it proved fraught with danger. In the forests of the snow-covered lowlands wild Slavic tribesmen lay in wait for them with poisoned arrows.

At last they arrived at the permanent snowfields. They had come to a terrain into which no one had ever before ventured. This abode of tranquillity and silence had remained undisturbed in the shadow of the snow for many thousands of years. Those of the party who were versed in the lore of dreams and omens realised, trembling, that they were now very close to the White Magus.

One day they came to a stream beneath whose waters drifted strange flowers of frozen crystal, and they knew that this must be the mountain on whose peak he lived. They continued their painful journey upwards, picking their way between fields of snow and rivers of ice. One by one the mules collapsed. The weakest members of the party became ill or suffered from terrifying hallucinations, and the group began to break up.

It was already night when its remaining members reached the Magus' ice gardens. In the astonishingly bright light of the stars they could see across enormous distances to the other peaks. Immense fields of ice stretched out before them, gleaming palely in the darkness. The cold was terrible. A blue light emanating from the palace itself flickered back and forth across the garden.

When they reached the top of the slippery stairway the Magus appeared at his gate to greet them. His austere, distinguished face made all petty thoughts seem shameful, and their bent, weary backs straightened as if under a reproach.

After listening attentively while the Archilogothetos explained the reason for their coming, he promised to visit the little Princess and do everything in his power to help her. It would be hard indeed to leave his astronomical tower and return to the bustling, petty-minded world from which he had grown so remote, but he respected both the moral code that required him to help all who turned to him and the law that made the Emperor the ruler of the world. While he remained in that world he would always follow his duty.

However, on that particular night certain very special events were about to be played out in the heavens, events to be witnessed only once in a hundred years, and which set the pattern for the next hundred, and he felt obliged to spend that one last night in his tower. Towards dawn, with a heavy heart, he bade farewell to the eternal stars.

The next day they set out for Byzantium. With the Magus at their side, the road was now very easy. He knew of pathways that led between the snowfields, and the Danube meekly allowed his longboat to ride on its back. Along the way he gladly dispensed advice to all who sought his counsel, treating everyone with the same kindliness and respect.

When they reached Drinapolis word came that Princess Zoë was on her deathbed. Alarmed and concerned, the Magus increased the pace of the journey. But by the time they arrived at the city walls of Byzantium the bells were already tolling. The Princess was dead.

The Emperor Constantine who received the Magus was a man broken by grief.

"If you had arrived just a few hours earlier, you might have saved her!"

"I am to blame," replied the crestfallen Magus. "If I had set out immediately I would have been here in time. Eternal shame upon my head!"

He entered the room where the body lay and examined it carefully. When he returned his expression was even more sombre.

"I do not believe I could have helped her while she was alive," he declared. "Your daughter must have been a very special person, my lord. It takes a most exceptional character to die of that most helpless form of love—pity. She froze to death because the children of the city were dying of cold, in their yearning for the lost sunlight of ancient Greece. It is a perilous thing to allow yourself to face life with a bared heart, not knowing, as one should, the need to abstract oneself from the world. You see, up there in my astronomical tower I can foretell every misfortune that blows down onto the world from the fateful stars. Should I ever allow pity to overwhelm me, if only for a moment, I would be dead within the hour. But the eternal winter of the Carpathians shields my heart. The sea of life cannot reach my tower, other than as a pure and rarified vapour. I could have done nothing for your daughter while she was still alive; and now that her heart is cold … but I have never yet made a wasted journey … "

Deep in thought, he wandered through the Palace gardens.

During the night he called again on the Emperor, who had remained beside his daughter's bier.

"My lord, I cannot leave with this business unfinished," he began. "I have decided to resort to the very greatest, and most dangerous, of all forms of magic, something a magus can work only once in his life—the art of raising the dead. I cannot reveal its many secrets and difficulties to you, but there is one problem you will have to find a way round by some means or another. You know that in this vale of woe everything happens at a cost, just as the great mystery of birth requires both pain and the shedding of blood. If I am to bring a dead person back to life there must be an exchange with someone still living. My lord, if I am to revive your daughter I shall need a volunteer for sacrifice."

"I am sure a great many people," the Emperor replied, "would be prepared to give their lives for her. The heart of the entire city beat in her breast. I would willingly die myself, but unfortunately affairs of state require my continuing existence."

The next day heralds let it be known throughout the town that they were looking for someone to lay down his or her life for the sake of the little Princess. "The life of the body is transient, but this person's name will live in grateful memory for ever."

But in all that city of stone, no one came forward. The fact that Zoë had died, and would never again be seen going to church in her long, trailing dress, did not concern them, and they probably did not even notice that their lives had become even more impoverished and oppressed than before.

The Magus had expected no less. He knew the people. He knew that their drab lives were so limiting they were incapable of giving anything for the sake of a greater cause.

He saw too that there was only one person, someone not caught up in petty concerns, whose life was indeed worthy of such a sacrifice, and that person was himself. It did not seem to him unreasonable or unfair that he should surrender his life for someone else, someone he did not know and whose existence had so far been a matter of perfect indifference to him. It was not as if he were someone who would one day be important. He too would have to die one day, and death was not something he feared. He had lived twice as long as people usually did. He already knew all there was to know, and more than was permitted to man. The world had no unredeemed promises left in store for him.

He communicated his decision to the Emperor, who was so astonished he was quite unable to find words to thank him.

A long-abandoned building in the Palace gardens was fitted out for the Magus. Guards were stationed all around so that no animal or human could come near. There he spent the night in acts of sorcery. The guards were convinced they could hear all sorts of voices inside. According to some of them, just before dawn the building was bathed in a strange blue light.

As soon as he woke the next morning, the Emperor called on the Magus. He found him sitting in a vast armchair in the middle of the empty room, a broken man. In a barely audible voice he announced:

"My lord, the great spell has done its work. Everything on earth and in heaven has assisted its aims. All that remains is for me to die."

"And what is your last wish, Magus?" the Emperor asked.

"I have no last wish, just as I had no first one. But my final instructions are these: to place the body of the little Princess on a white bier, clad in the full ceremonial robes of a lady of noble birth, and carry it at midday down to the square outside the Cathedral. There you must set down my body too, on a black bier, and that is where the miracle of life and death will take place. Live happily, my lord."

All routine work in the city came to a halt. Too inflamed with curiosity even to eat, the citizens put on their finest clothes. With trembling hands Zoë's former attendants dressed her corpse in the formal, pure-gold coronation robes a woman was permitted to don just once in her life. On her head they placed the huge, heavy diadem. In inexpressible excitement, the Emperor knelt before the crucifix.

All this time the Magus had remained sitting in his armchair. When the final moment came, he dispatched his soul to its last and greatest exaltation. One after another, his vital organs failed, and with them faded all the soft sensory impressions, the sounds, scents and images of the transient world. Then even the sense of weariness ceased, and the soul unfurled its wings on a loftier, freer, plane. An irresistible lightness carried it ever upwards, ever higher and higher—the light grew ever brighter, the boundaries of the soul ever wider. It now floated on a sea of light, the one men call the Sea of Forgetting, for when the soul comes there it can no longer remember that it was ever anywhere else, the Eternal Present floods it with a wondrous sense of peace, and the hideous shackles that constitute the sense of 'I am' fall away.

And then his soul stood trembling on the final shore. He had come this far before, but always fallen back again, able to proceed no further. Normally this moment of pause would occur in the same instant as the soul's ascent and be immeasurably brief, since the strength and desire that had propelled it on its way were great enough for it to break through the boundary, taking it on to a second sea, the one men call Death.

Meanwhile the body the Magus had left behind had been washed and laid out, according to his instructions, on a black bier, and the procession set off on its way to the accompaniment of slow dirges.

But his soul continued its upward flight, leaving immensities incomprehensible to human understanding far below. And now it was no longer alone. All round it appeared a multitude of spirits clad in light, and the sun's coach, with its wheel of golden spokes, stood glittering before it.

The soul of the White Magus stepped up into the coach, in which were gathered before him a host of other sages, magi and masters of the lore of the stars. They thronged around him, rejoicing, holding him in place, and he was able briefly to rest.

Then the soul moved to the very edge of the sun coach and looked back at the way it had come, across immeasurable distances all the way down to the earth. There it lay, a grey, lax, languid, motionless object, far, far below. It was not a comforting sight, and the soul prepared to journey further on.

Then suddenly, from one particular spot on the Earth, a sort of luminosity flared up. It was quite unlike the celestial radiance of heaven, but worldly, opaque, and deeply disturbing. As the soul's vision slowly adjusted to the distance, it realised that the light was coming from the city of Byzantium.

It saw a great multitude standing before the cathedral, around a white bier, and on the bier lay the miraculous form of a young woman, the source of the strange earthly radiance. Then, very slowly, the girl sat up, then stood fully erect. The ceremonial golden robes that enveloped her, denoting her high birth, glowed like a chalice. Now she was all the Magus' soul could see. It watched as her arms began slowly to move, like the arms of a person walking in sleep. Never before had it beheld anything like this.

Then suddenly it could see everything, as the earthly light spread out in all directions, enveloping the whole world as it slept in the midday sun, its radiant face adorned with a million triumphantly verdant trees and flowers … and the sea was as blue as the sky, the sky was as deep as the sea, and where they met the breezes softly caressed the fledgling waves.

And the Magus' soul was filled with sorrow that it had never seen any of these things before. It leant out over the edge of the sun's coach. The running board was made of gold and very slippery, the distance below was beyond measuring, the soul was overcome with vertigo and fell headlong, plunging ever downwards towards earth. Liberated from the body, it was driven by a single gravitational force—desire.

The soul of the White Magus hurtled down through myriad worlds, back into his abandoned body. In the tower of the great cathedral known as the Hagia Sophia, the bells were tolling twelve.

The crowd standing around the little Princess watched as, very slowly, the royal maiden held up a hand in front of her, as if to fend off the sunlight. She was alive!

Suddenly someone gave a great shout and pointed in horror to the other bier, the black one, on which lay the body of the Magus. And then everyone gazed in awe as the right hand of the dead Magus slowly stroked his brow. In the same instant the little Princess' right hand fell back, under its own dead weight.

The silence, and the horror, were indescribable. Slowly, very slowly, the White Magus raised his head, with its huge crown of white hair, and at the same time Princess Zoë's head drooped, like the head of a broken lily. Slowly the Magus sat up, as she slumped down on her knees. Like a ghost or supernatural apparition, he rose to his feet, while she lay down on the white bier. He gave a great sigh and spread his arms out wide, as the Princess clutched her hands to her breast, like a statue on the lid of a coffin. His eyes opened fully, and his appalled gaze met that of the Princess—in its very last half-second of life. Then her eyes closed for ever.

The great bells tolled. In the stunned silence of the pitiless midday sun the crowd fell to their knees and beat their breasts, though none knew why. Very few noticed that the Magus had leapt down from his bier, thrown himself on the ground, and was sobbing like a child.

As the little Princess lay on her bier, the diadem slowly slipped from her forehead, and the eternal sun of ancient Greece wove flowers of gold in her radiant hair.

1923

AJÁNDOK'S BETROTHAL

Saint John of the Flowers,
how bright is your night
as I stand here before you,
in simple reverence—
till your clear bright skies
grow sombre with clouds.

IT WAS ST JOHN'S NIGHT, the night of Saint John of the Flowers, the shortest night of the year, when darkness crouches low on its ankles before rising slowly, slowly, to its full height once again.

The wagon of the Great Bear had already been wheeled out, freshly washed, into the sky, and the entire village, both young and old, in all their festive finery, flocked up the hill to where the statue of the Blessed Virgin stood wreathed in flowers. At its feet they made a pile of straw and brushwood and, at the appointed hour, set it alight in the time-honoured fashion. The straw flickered with a young, skittering flame, as did the glowing cheeks of young Lidi as she was led into the centre, and soon the brushwood followed, slow and hesitant, like the dancing of the older women, and the fire of flowery Saint John was fully ablaze.

The next instant, from every hilltop far and near, answering fires flashed out greetings to one another, like

so many kings of the summer throned in radiance above
the wide plains.

Along one side of the conflagration sat the worthy
elders, among them the miller, as proud as if the whole
summer were his own, for the entire harvest was piled
high in his barn. On the other side the venerable older
women, including the miller's mother—renowned
for her wisdom in seven villages—sat looking across
to where the comely younger women were seated.
With these was her oldest granddaughter, the same
Lidi, whose gaze was directed in turn to where the
handsome young men of the village were seated.
Among them was Bálint, the miller's foreman, her
secret sweetheart.

The boys all carried long sticks with lengths of straw
attached to the ends. These were now set alight and
brandished overhead in waving, snake-like movements,
leaping nightmarishly in all directions, while the girls
threw their fresh flowers onto the fire. The young people
shouted and danced, until the blaze finally settled down
to burn with a gentle, steady flame (Saint John's bonfire
never did last very long) and then the games began. A
handful of the girls set the song in motion, and the rest
quickly followed:

> *Tűz villog, nap ragyog*
> *hunyor a személye,*
> *rózsa nyílik előtte*
> *és utána liliom*

Fire burns, sun shines
incarnate in the hellebore,
the rose opens before it
and after it the lily

and Lidi said to Bálint, and Bálint said to Lidi: "You
are my treasure," and all the young people shrieked
with laughter, as if hearing this news for the first time.
Bálint muttered something under his breath, then rose
to his feet, as did the furiously blushing Lidi, and there
they stood, side by side, an acknowledged couple. They
waited while the girls sang the wooing song, then jumped,
hand in hand, through the fire. The miller just smiled
and smiled, thinking of his grandchildren as budding ears
of corn in God's great field—there would be so many
children, a happy family in the old windmill, and he
would be prouder than the Emperor himself when the
guard paraded before him.

The embers clung to their waning life, and the couples
leapt through it one after another in response to the
changing lines of the song. Then when everyone had
taken Saint John's blessing, the lads came to a stop facing
the girls. One of the younger girls would now have to run
between the lines shouting, "Lidi Miller's house is burning,
put it out, put it out". She would then be followed by all
the publicly acknowledged couples, starting with the last
in line, the girl running ahead of the boy. But when the
boys got themselves in position to set off down the line,
they realised that none of the younger girls were where
they should have been. They had all been sent home to

bed, in order not to lose face. The only ones left standing opposite their partners and waiting to run were those already betrothed. Just one unattached girl remained on the scene, a mere child, the miller's youngest daughter, aged fifteen. Her grandmother had sent her over with instructions to run down the line shouting the required words so that the couples would not be disappointed. She approached with a smile on her face that was a joy to see—but as she grew closer, and cast her eye over the many fine young men standing there with their partners, she burst into tears and ran away, sulking.

Few of the villagers, being all (the women especially) so busy with their plans and dreaming up little love nests for the couples, can have spared a thought for that one little girl among all the others, now wandering somewhere out of sight, alone. The song and the games continued, nor did the miller's old mother forget to bake the ceremonial herbs over the flames, and the revels went on until suddenly it was very late, and with the next day's labours in mind they all set off homewards.

Ajándok—for that was the little girl's name—was the late-born child of elderly parents. She wandered through the gardens, not bothering to dry her weeping eyes, her lips red from sulking and her mouth turned down, reluctant to venture as far as the main road. It was a wonderfully clear night, full of palpitating stars, with not a single cloud in all its pathless expanse. Peering through hedges, she could make out, here and there, broken-down old people sitting in the porches in front of their houses, their faces gazing up at the shining galaxies. Even the dogs were silent. Perhaps they had all gone off to celebrate in some other place, where their kind have a seat at their masters' bone-covered tables. At the far end stood the windmill, its huge four-armed sails motionless, as under a spell, with not a whisper of wind to drive them.

"Perhaps I should just throw myself in the river," the child thought sadly. "The fishermen would haul me up in their nets before dawn, with golden fishes in my hair, and lay my body out in the market square, and everyone would come and cry over me, and a rich and powerful man would take me back to the village in a golden coach, and my parents would wail and weep, and say: 'She was such a little thing when she was alive, and now she's dead, and she was the most beautiful of all of them.' And a hundred young men would come and stare at me, but it would be too late, my mouth would be cold and white, and I would be all cold and white, as white as a lily."

Ajándok was indeed beautiful, as beautiful as fairy gossamer, soft and supple, with long golden hair. But she was still very young, not yet marriageable, not at all ready to be led away as a bride. And she was as solitary as a river by night. She gazed long and thoughtfully at her barely rounded arms, thinking of the future bridegroom she would one day cradle in them—the young man who had only now set out across unimaginably distant seas, his road beset by every sort of terror—and she grieved that the lamp in her eyes could never cast its beam to that faraway place because it was running out of oil and, one night soon, would die out altogether.

She had now reached the silent mill. It lay in darkness. The sight of its mute sails deepened her loneliness and made the far-off stranger seem even more hopelessly remote. Somewhere in its kitchen darkness was preparing dinner, and oh! she wished, if only the mill could suddenly launch itself into the sky above the fields, like a terrifying bird of the night, clanking and rattling as it flew, and reach heaven by dawn! In heaven, among the golden clouds ... that was where she would find her rest.

A merry din was heard as everyone—the miller, his mother, Lidi, Bálint, the serving girls and the young workmen—came banging their way up the wooden stairs and into the mill. The long table was already laid and waiting. There was to be a double celebration that night, for the moment they arrived at the front door Bálint had gone up to the miller, doffed his cap and asked for Lidi's hand in marriage. There had been none of the customary sending of an apple, or a woman with two oven mops, or the man with the flask of wine: this suitor had no need of such tokens—the couple had understood one another quite long enough. Nor was there any of the ritual wrangling between the families, just handshakes all round, the men crowding round Bálint to pump his hand and the women showering Lidi with kisses. Ajándok went over, fell on her older sister's neck in tears, then promptly ran out of the room.

After waiting a suitable length of time for her to calm down and become more amenable, her grandmother went to see how she was. She tracked her down to the woodshed, where she was sitting on a pile of logs.

"Why are you crying, my pretty flower? Tell me why."

Ajándok made no answer. She did not know what to say. She just clung to her granny's shoulder while the sobs shook her like a winnowing sieve.

"My little one, my blessed girl, don't cry. Haven't you got a lovely father to guide your thoughts, and your beautiful older sister, see, who's now become engaged? Who ever saw anyone cry on such a wonderful day? You have everything you could possibly want. You've got your pussy-cat Mirók, the little scamp, with a silk ribbon round his neck, and your lovely shock-headed doll Faraj. Nobody sends you out into the fields at dawn to sweep up the gleanings. You live like the fairy Ilona. You aren't like any of the other girls. You have lovely blonde hair, my angel, and the colour of the ever-faithful forget-me-not in your eyes. Your skin is finer, your bones are more delicate than other people's, and we take such good care to shelter you from the sun, and the wind, and nasty words that put a curse on you —so you really mustn't cry."

Ajándok replied: "It's no use—not even if Mirók and Lidi, and Faraj, and all the treasures of the fairy Ilona were tucked under my pillow … Granny, I'm so alone in this big wide world."

"Ah, now I see. So the little girl would like to be a big girl, is that right, my little lily-of-the-valley? I know only too well what a bitter thing it is to be single on flowery Saint John's Night and not have a young man. At times like this a girl is like a look-out tree. There she stands, all alone, naked to the wind, gazing around the wide meadow for days on end, waiting for the time for when she will finally be fed with the sweet food of the heart … and then, just before dawn, she hears the neighing of horses telling someone: 'That's where the miller's beautiful daughter lives'—and the bridegroom enters, with dust on his boots, and a diamond-studded whip in his hand."

"Granny … if you really know everything … tell me when he will come, and what sort of man he will be."

The old lady became serious.

"You are asking me a very big thing, my flower. It's not for us to look for short cuts to find out what the future will bring in its own good time. But you know there is a way to do it, and it's lucky that you ask me this question on Saint John's Night, because it's the best time for every sort of magic. So keep your ears open, my girl, and make the sign of the cross, in case some passing evil spirit should overhear our conversation and draw near."

Ajándok did as she was told. She could feel the magic of the night, and the dark air closing in around her filled with unseen presences, all just waiting for her to turn her back or shut her eyes for a second, when they would poke their fearsome great heads out at her.

"Now listen carefully, my girl. You must go up to the very top of the mill, to the wheel that drives the sails. There, at the bottom of a large chest, you will find all the lengths of ceremonial herbs and grasses I have dried over the fire on previous Saint John's Nights. Gather them up into a little bundle and bring it down with you. On the stroke of midnight, you must leave the mill and, whatever happens to you then, do not look behind you but go straight to the old ruined well. There, you must say three

Hail Marys over the water, lie down beside the rim, and place the bundle under your head. You will then fall asleep, and you will sleep just as you would in your own bed. Pay very careful attention to your dreams, because the person you see in your dreams will be the bridegroom you long for. Do as I say, and be sure to forget none of what I have told you."

Ajándok wiped away her tears and set off for the attic at the top of the mill. She had never liked going up there, not even by day: but this was Saint John's Night, after all. It was a fearful place. Here, it was said, the mad young mill-worker Gergely had hanged himself. The winding staircase seemed to go on for ever in the darkness, twisting and turning all the way. At every landing it was as if someone had been sitting there just a moment before and then fled noisily up another flight. After countless turnings and twistings she reached the round window, the huge Cyclops eye of the mill. She thought of those evenings in her childhood, all those times when on her way home from the fields she had seen some creature stick its terrifying head out of the window, then draw it back … perhaps someone was lurking there now? But she gathered up her strength and peered out through it. Down below lay the empty fields. Between the clusters of pitch-black trees, and as far as the most distant seas, the world was utterly deserted. As she sat there, on the staircase that went on for ever, the little girl's heart beat in total isolation.

Then, just a few steps higher, stumbling and very close to tears, she felt a wave of dizziness. She snapped her

LOVE IN A BOTTLE

mouth shut, and suddenly—she nearly screamed—she bumped into something. It was the attic door. After an awkward scraping it gave way to the pressure of her hands. As she entered her nose was assaulted by the smell of musty old jumble. She was surrounded by unfamiliar objects, each demanding its due, its toll of pure terror.

"Courage, Ajándok. The heroines of fairy stories have braved far more terrifying tunnels on the path to the diamond-studded gates. It was an altogether different Ajándok, now defiant and sinister to behold, who ran unsteadily over the creaking floorboards in the blue light shed by the thin, fruitless ploughings of the moon that added to her fear. An unseen joist blocked her way, almost jumping up at her, and she had to step over it as over a dead animal. It was followed by what looked like another. Seeing it, she leapt back and sat down hard on the joist. Something was hanging from this second beam, a black, lumpish mass. Her heart fluttered like the wings of a lost bird, as her tearful eyes slowly made out that this object, the source of so much alarm, was nothing more than a haunch of ham hung up to be smoked.

Without knowing how she managed it, she eventually found herself at last in the centre of the boarded space where the great chest stood. She rummaged through the pile of old clothes, calendars and household jumble, gathered up the herbs in her trembling hands, stuffed them into her bag, gave a deep sigh and started on her way back. Fear gripped her once again, even though the situation was now a little less desperate. At what seemed an immense distance down below she could now make out the light from the fireplace, signalling that there would at some point be an end to her frightful journey. But she was still a good few paces from the door when her feet froze in terror, rooting her to the spot.

She had heard a whirring, rustling sort of noise, and it made her flesh creep the way it does when someone stares at us from behind. But she dared not turn round. She was incapable of movement. The moon held her body trapped between its narrow spikes, and she stood there like a person bewitched. Very slowly, as in a nightmare, she managed to force herself round, and immediately clapped her hand to her eyes. This was no dream. Beneath the cloth sail of the windmill stood the pitch-black figure of a man, with something held tight under his arm. Ajándok screamed. The mysterious figure gave a sudden start, flitted away between the sails, and vanished.

Still clutching her bundle, Ajándok ran back down to her room. People begged, demanded, to know what had happened. But she had no words to describe her terror.

Now they were all seated around the table. The vapour from the warm wine had lifted everyone's spirits, and the sight of the two keys, one for the bride's old home and one for the new, had driven away all thoughts of night. Kindliness shone in everyone's eyes, and their laughter wore festive garments.

There was a knocking at the door. Silence fell, and people were still trying to decide who this very late visitor might be when he finally entered. The unexpected caller was a figure clad in black, his boots covered in dust, with a large book bound in pigskin clutched under his arm. His cloak—which looked wide enough to drive clouds along with—hung down all round him, like the folded wings of a raven. Indeed his whole aspect was that of a great wind-blown bird, and his voice, when he spoke, was low and hoarse with the dust of the highways of seven counties.

"My name is Máté the scholar. I am one of the paupers of the famous order of Saint Lazarus. I am a wanderer, good people, and exhausted from a long journey. I must ask you for a place to sleep this fine night, and a little milk, and a loaf of bread, since I cannot pay you for them."

The miller was a hospitable and jovial man, and he made the pauper of Saint Lazarus take his seat at the table, though he did not particularly relish this sort of visitor. And indeed, although the scholar filled his place at a corner of the table quietly enough, there was little about him of the cheerfulness that filled his neighbours. It was as if his black cloak cast its shadow over the entire table, like some huge-winged buzzard hovering over the courtyard killing the joy of the merry chickens, and after his arrival the conversation became rather subdued. The talk was all of plans for the wedding, finding a best man who would also be a skilful rhymester, and calculating just how much wine would have to be ordered. They tried to draw the wandering scholar in, but to no avail. He heard them out, but in a manner that suggested he had never known what the words 'wedding', 'bride' or 'happiness' might mean.

For all that, the old lady took good care of him. She set down a fresh, uncut loaf of bread before him, and a full mug of milk. It was Saint John's Night, and she knew what she was doing. He fell to, but ate very strangely, not as a Hungarian would. He scrutinised the loaf from one side and then the other, and sniffed the milk cautiously before every sip, as if afraid that they were about to poison him. Meanwhile he spoke not a word, and looked to neither left nor right.

Nor did he notice that there was someone who never stopped staring at him. It was his immediate neighbour, Ajándok. From the very first glance the little girl's heart had taken pity on the wandering scholar—this poor, uncouth, abandoned vagrant with thorns clinging to his clothes from his wanderings in distant forests. Finding a creature beside her who seemed even more of an orphan than she felt herself to be, sad little Ajándok's sorrow began to dissolve, and her kindly heart longed to comfort him.

The scholar finally noticed her when she leant over to him to put some sugar in his milk. His first response was to cover the mug with his hand in terror; but then he acquiesced, and even thanked her.

"No one ever puts sugar in my milk," he observed plaintively. "I always have it without. But sugar is very good, if you can get it."

"But if you want it, why don't you ask?"

"Me, ask for sugar? I'm afraid that wouldn't go down well with the master."

"But when you find a good master, who looks kindly on you?"

"I've met very few of those. I know I look like a scarecrow. But I don't ask for much. All I want is a bite to eat and somewhere to lay my head. When people oblige I never thank them, and if they don't they live to regret it. I just keep moving on—there are plenty of other villages and my legs are long. I never sit anywhere long enough to warm my seat."

Sensing the miller's gaze fully upon him, he stopped.

"So where are you from, master scholar?" was the question. The scholar behaved as if he hadn't heard.

Soon enough, people lost interest in him, their thoughts full of their own happy plans.

But Ajándok fussed around him even more devotedly, finding a cushion for him to sit on, as if he were a specially honoured guest, cutting his bread for him and pouring his milk into her own ornately decorated mug. He even managed to thank her, in his scarcely audible voice. She blushed at this display of magnanimity, and gazed at him with such a loving look that he reddened slightly in return—the faint glowing of embers beneath a layer of ash.

"Have you come very far?" she suddenly asked, timidly.

"I certainly have," he replied. "Through seven forests, from the land of seven cities. In Transylvania I studied up to the thirteenth grade … I lived in a cave with twelve companions … a dark cave, with bears and owls … we were barely human ourselves … and the nights were bitter cold … Then we moved on … crossing over flimsy footbridges … carrying torches … up into the heart of the mountain."

His speech came in fragments, as if he wanted to drop the subject at every turn but was unable to withstand Ajándok's loving gaze. "In the heart of the mountain we came upon a threshing wheel … we stopped before it, all thirteen of us … we knew one of us would have to die … either myself or one of the others … so we all climbed up and stood on it … and it started to turn … then suddenly, 'Jaj!'—my best friend fell … he screamed at us as he lay there among the whirling blades … it was all up for him … But we survived … twelve of us now … and now we could go … anywhere in the world we wanted … for whatever foolish reason. But this is not a fit story for you, my little sister. It'll give you bad dreams."

"Never mind that—tell me more. Where did you go after that?"

"Where did I go? I couldn't tell you the number of countries—you would be an old maid, my dear little sister, by the time you'd heard it all. As King Solomon said: 'To grow in wisdom is to grow in suffering.' The fact is, since I first held this book under my arm I've not had a moment's rest. The breeze starts to rise just before dawn, and I think, perhaps on the slopes of some faraway hill there'll be a fountain of wine to quench my thirst; or in some snowy cave of ice, who knows? perhaps I might at last have my wish and get some sleep, and find what I need—a longboat waiting for me on the shore of the Óperencián sea to take me to my rest on the eternal waves. So long as there are country roads under my feet, I shall never find rest."

Ajándok asked, rather petulantly, why he had come there if the world was so much wider elsewhere.

"Everyone who goes wandering, my little sister, does so because there's somewhere he wants to get to. The end of the world is just that, the end of the world, and they say that once you get there you will be able to find rest. When I finally reached this wide plain I saw this mill standing in the distance and I felt happier than I had for years. My dear little sister, you are a miller's daughter, you can never have known how wonderful it is to be no longer pursued by the wind, when you have lost the power of your wings and are sleeping under the open sky … and suddenly there stands the mill, with its sails."

It had grown very late. Wishing one another a peaceful good night, people rose from the table. Lidi's cheeks burnt in anticipation of the promised kisses that the autumn would bring, and everyone knew that her dream of Bálint would be one of roses. All that awaited Ajándok was the cold bed of a child.

The old lady led the scholar Máté to his sleeping place, a bench covered with sheepskin. He stretched himself out along it, pulled his cloak over him, and in that manner fell instantly and soundly asleep.

Silence pervaded the entire mill. The chairs and long table could now stretch out and rest too. Soft, rustling sounds were heard. The happy dreams of warm bodies came to life. Down the cracked and crannied chimney, over the hearth, in and out of the mountains of grey ash, those dreams, the miracles and nightmares of flowery Saint John's Eve, glided silently.

Then the great bell tolled. It seemed determined to flood the whole plain with its outpouring. Twelve o'clock.

Ajándok rose, pulled on her dress, took out the bundle, and tiptoed out of the mill.

The moon was so bright it was like a second day, in a whiter, more silent world where the flowers were less lush. But she did not look behind her, and as she stepped out she no longer felt afraid, and her grief melted away. She felt sure that on just such a moonlit night, in a landscape sent down from another world, the person she was expecting would be sure to appear.

And there stood the well. Inside its crumbling rim the frogs croaked their ancient watery songs. It was said that the well was as ancient as the mill, and the mill was so old that even to think how old it was would take for ever.

She said the three Hail Marys, put the bundle down beside the well, rested her head on it and savoured the smell of the roasted herbs. And there she lay for a long, long time, in great peace, as if on her own bed. On her white brow the nimble fingers of tiny dreams spun a bridal wreath … until, after who knows how long, or when she became aware of it … there was a man standing next to the well, a tall, pitch-black figure, his eye raised heavenwards in rapture. The moon stroked his face with its soft hands, and made him as handsome as the prince of some far-off Western land.

She stood up. She knew. This man was her bride-groom.

It was the scholar.

She went up to him, and without knowing what she was doing—she was still in a dream—took his hand. With unhurried deliberation, like someone taking a vow, she declared: "You are my betrothed."

He gave a start, then stared at her as if she were a miraculous being risen from the well. "Is that what you want, Ajándok?"

"It's not I who want it. I don't want anything. It was the magic that brought me to you, by night, on flowery Saint John's Night. You are the man I was told I would see. My husband-to-be."

"As you say, Ajándok. It is true. It was no chance wind that brought me to this place. But all the same—do you know who I am?"

"You are a wanderer, and a weary one, seeking rest. I know that you are my bridegroom."

"But think about this carefully, Ajándok, and may God bless you. You see this book under my arm? In it you may read terrible things. And I am the one who frightened you earlier, in the attic—it was my way into the house."

"God bless that moment!"

"But I am not an ordinary person. No girl has ever loved me. I am a vagrant. I don't know how to live in one place!"

"You are my husband: I shall follow you everywhere."

"Ajándok, wonderful things do happen in this world. The wind racing by will sometimes turn and send a bunch of flowers spinning to the ground; hurricanes will crouch down and play among the corn stalks, like children. And," he shouted, "I do believe that you are my betrothed, that you will stay with me for ever, and I shall never wander again." He fell to his knees and kissed the hem of her garment.

"All my wanderings have been for your sake, Ajándok, my betrothed. Because of you I have carried the dust of the road of every land on my shoes. You are the clearing, the open glade in which I can rest at last. You are the long-lost palace to which I am now returning, the bed in which I shall finally sleep; the scarf that will seel my ever-watchful eyes; the little nest that will calm my beating wings; the golden chain that will fetter my flying feet. I have finally found what I have always been looking for, and now the mill will always be there for me, the mill and its sails!"

Ajándok could only listen in silence and let the kisses fall on her happy hand. She was in another world, where one drank the fragrant milk of moon-white cows.

Then the scholar drew himself up and said, almost fearfully: "I have one last journey to make, Ajándok, through the village. Thus it is written in my book. And then ... I shall throw away the book and never travel again. Will you come with me on that one last journey, my betrothed?"

"Of course I shall."

Hand in hand they raced down the little hill on which the mill stood, and into the village. From house to house, courtyard to courtyard, they ran in silence, nor did the dogs bark at them. Then the scholar began to exercise his miraculous craft. The moment he reached a farmyard he would lift up his book and begin to read (he could see the words even in the dark). In it was written the name of the owner, and what sort of man he was—according to which the scholar proceeded to reward or punish him. There was one who was envious and quarrelsome: the scholar blew behind the left ear of his cow, and from then on its calf would drink blood along with its milk, and in no time at all his entire young stock was destroyed. At the next place the owner was a good man, and there the scholar blew behind the cow's right ear, and thereafter the milk would be rich, the calf it suckled would grow well, and the faces of his children would be ruddy with health. He also wrought justice by means of the pigs. The bad farmer's pig had its tail twisted slightly, and no bacon or ham ever came from that pig, for by the autumn it was dead. If he made a baleful sign on a fruit tree, it would be impossible to rid it of caterpillars: the sign simply brought forth wave after wave of new ones. But where he left a favourable sign the tree would produce fine fruit, so lush you could hardly bear to sink your teeth into it. The bad farmer's land he scattered with salt, and it became saline and produced nothing. Over the good man's land he made a sign with his staff, whereupon the mice gave it a wide berth and hail never struck it. Thus he went from house to house, like a nocturnal bishop on his rounds.

Meanwhile, in the intimate language of plighted lovers, the two of them built up their plans for their future life together. The was no doubt in the scholar's mind that the miller would grant him his daughter's hand, and he took it for granted that he would be rich. He knew that out in the marshland there was a hidden treasure, guarded by black dogs. He was the only person who understood their tongue, and they would allow him access to it. They agreed that the house of Máté the scholar would be built directly opposite the mill. It would not be an ordinary house, but a tower with a flat roof, and on it the two of them would sit out, on evenings just like this, and smile as they talked about times past, when the scholar was still a vagrant wandering the highways and Ajándok was a young girl, playing with her dolls and too young for marriage. Their cows would have glass bells hanging from their necks; they would never have to shout at their servants—when summoned they would obey in perfect silence; Ajándok would walk on tiptoe round the bedroom, and the door wouldn't squeak; when their saucepans banged together they would make music, and Mirók the kitten would sit in pride of place on a tower of cushions. Their front door would be forever open, and all sorts of vagrants would come and stay with them, but because of these visitors they would often not leave the house for weeks, and on Sundays they would do nothing but just sit there gazing at each other, and Ajándok would say: "See, here I am at home, the children are growing up, and when my beloved comes back they will be as tall as he is," and Máté the scholar would add: "See, here I am at home. The country roads were bumpy and hard going, but now the earth has grown soft and rich, the highways are behind me, and I can rest."

Thus, in a shared waking dream, they built their house of air: the vagrant looking to have a roof over his head and his betrothed, the child Ajándok; and both believed they really would live in it. Confidently they made their way through the sleeping village, and the scholar brought blushes from his bride's cheek by talking of the little one they would one day have. His hair would be blond, like his mother's. He would not come into the world, as his father had, with his teeth fully developed: in fact he wouldn't be like him at all, but calm and church-going, and the blessing of the holy water of baptism would shine on his brow for ever. The old ladies of the village would dandle him on their knees, and angels would sing to him. He would be truly beautiful, the king of all his little companions.

In the heart of the village, just outside the church, they stopped, Máté the scholar and Ajándok, to exchange tokens. Ajándok was still too young to own a beautiful embroidered scarf, so she simply gave him the ribbon she tied in the hair of Faraj her doll.

"But what can I give you, Ajándok? I had a veil, made of gossamer, which I once bought from a peddler who was two hundred years old, and other little knick-knacks too, but I used the gossamer to bind a wound, and I gave the knick-knacks away in one place or another on my way here, before I got to you, and now I have nothing to give my betrothed. Do you know what, Ajándok? I shall give you this book. You don't yet know how to use it; I am the only one who knows how to do that. But … when I have a home, what need will I have of it then, and what will my loss of wisdom mean to anyone? I shall give it to you—when we get to the end of the village."

The child waiting to be born rushed up to them, his tiny hands raised in the air. The cheerful babble filled their hearts with a feeling of benevolence, and they stood there, the pride and joy of the village.

But the night was waning, and they still had a way to go. Here and there the first faint colours were already dappling the white walls of the houses, and the air was chill.

They went on to within a stone's throw of the end of the village. There they stopped outside a house with a fearsome reputation. The owner was a wicked man, drunk and boorish, the associate of thieves. Ajándok drew closer to her betrothed. She no longer felt anger now towards the malefactor because, in her dream, she knew her husband would take good care of her; and they now had a child, a beautiful child with large, beautiful eyes.

Then the scholar opened his book, and studied it for a long time. Slowly the colour drained from his face. He slumped against the sharp fence, beat his brow and looked distraught for what seemed an age, then he suddenly seized the terrified Ajándok by the shoulder and demanded: "Ajándok, what shall we call our child?"

In her terror she could not reply.

"His name will be Never Was, because we never shall have children. Get up. Clear off out of here. We shall never see each other again!"

Then he collapsed in misery against the fence. Ajándok just stood there, wringing her hands. She felt everything slipping away through her fingers.

The scholar looked up at her. "Are you still here, Ajándok? It's no use. It's written here. I can't help it. And even if I tried, it would be no use. There are even more terrible things in this book, and even worse things inside me. Off you go, Ajándok, and pray for my soul. Pray for the damned."

Ajándok stood shivering in the chilly dawn, then buried herself in his arms: "I shall never leave you, I shall never ever leave you!"

And though her blood froze in her veins when she saw what would have to be, she did not move from his side. But he never spared her a glance. Pulling his cloak around him, he stepped quietly up to the window of the house. Inside lay the child, sleeping open-mouthed in its cot. The scholar pressed his deathly pale face against the window and stared boldly into the room: his glance was so terrible and so fierce that Ajándok steeled herself to place her hand in front of his eyes to protect the child, before she realised that that terrible look would have bored right through her bloodless fingers. Dreadful minutes passed while he continued to stare; then the child woke and gazed at the window in wide-eyed astonishment. Suddenly its two eyes darkened, and it burst into a faltering, abandoned cry. The cry produced sounds of movement inside the house, the scholar seized Ajándok and hauled her after him as he ran. They ran like murderers being driven off with iron forks.

The rim of the sky was already pale, and a great cloud was passing solemnly overhead, like a dragon emerging from a swamp, as they do at the approach of sunrise. The air was heavy, as before a storm, when the trees dare not move but huddle with hunched shoulders, awaiting judgement. They finally stopped a little way beyond the village, where the marshland began. The scholar sat down on a boundary stone and spoke:

"See, I pass back and forth over the land like a hailstorm. I am a thing of ill omen, the secret horror of whispered prayers. Ajándok, many times in the past you have been terrified by the mere sound of my name, but to set eyes on me is a truly fearful thing. People cross themselves when they see me. So you should know: I am a *garabonciás*, a wandering scholar with occult powers. People drive me away with long whips. I do not want to do what I do, and perhaps it would be better if I didn't, in truth, because, my God! sometimes my lungs are left gasping for breath. So, poor little Ajándok, do you still love me?"

She answered: "You are my betrothed!"

Filled with sadness, he continued: "Look, Ajándok, it is already dawn. The wind is rising. There will be a storm, and I am awaited. No mortal girl has ever loved me. Ajándok, let us exchange a kiss, just once, so that I know how it tastes, and through it I shall hold you in my memory for ever. For who knows whether we shall ever see each other again."

"We cannot exchange kisses before we have exchanged tokens. Give me your book. I shall lock it well away, and look after it carefully, in a safe, safe place. Tell me you will never wander more; that we will make our home in the tower-house, as you promised, and be the pride and joy of the village."

"Dear little Ajándok, ask whatever you want—the golden lamb of the imperial princess, the diamond ring from the ear of the shaman's horse, Sleeping Beauty's enchanted bed—I shall set any one of these down before you for the sake of a single kiss. But I cannot give you the book. I know that now, and everything else is a lie. The book must always be mine. I can no more be free of it than I can be free of what I am."

"You must give me either the book, or nothing!"

"Well, then … yes … I see, that's how it must be—I shall never know what it is to be kissed by a mortal girl. But the tower-house, and the idea of living in it … how could I ever have believed that? The sun is coming up— gentle Saint John's Night is over. Thank you for coming with me on this one journey, Ajándok."

She burst into tears. So far her tears had been those of a child, without real meaning. Now the child Ajándok wept every one of her grown woman's tears.

"Ajándok, don't cry," he said. "You see, I am the one who should be crying. It is far better for you this way. I cannot share my life with anyone. I might blind you by looking you too fiercely in the eye; your frail skeleton would shatter in my embrace; our children would have been changelings, born with beards. It was cruel misfortune that we ever met, and there is nothing we can do about it. For sure, the wanderer will never find a home, or the orphan a mate."

Then the wind started up again. Something—a mass of something crouched low, a ball with a foot in the shape of a thorn bush—came scuttling down the highway, whipped along by the wind.

"Nini, devil's chariot!" shouted the scholar. "My faithful companion, my one true friend, here you come again, sent as a messenger by the storm! The open road, the joys of the full gallop, await me! I feel my wings growing back; by evening I shall have reached the city. I shall sleep at the top of the church tower and at midnight I shall ring the bells and make my escape on the back of a bull I have made mad, then I shall plunge into the swamp and tomorrow I shall be in Mauritania, under a blazing sun."

The wild windstorm gave its answer, throwing the dust from the nearby road in his eyes. But every speck of dust that flew into them struck a spark as from flint. His body expanded with every gust of air, straining to leave the earth behind, like the flames that hover flickering over the bonfire of someone possessed by the devil. And, like an organ freed into sound by a master, his voice boomed out, edged with sardonic laughter, terrible to hear.

"See, Ajándok, see! They're turning! The sails of the windmill are turning, driven by the wind! Let it drive me away, too, for I am a wandering scholar possessed by the devil, the son of a witch, raised by dragons, and this is my home, under stormy skies."

A mighty cloud of dust enveloped the huge black figure, as he ran off whooping down the highway, pursuing the battle that raged, howling, in the heavens.

Ajándok rose, wiped away her tears, and set off homewards. Her face was calm, serious—the face of one whose heart has been pierced by seven daggers. The storm tore at her frail body but could not break the flower of love in her, a flower that would never wilt.

That day, and for many years after, there was much talk in the village of the wandering scholar who put the wind in the windmill's sails, who went through the village on Saint John's Night and bewitched the heart of the poor little outlawed girl. Miraculous things were told of him even after he had left. There were those who met him on the highway, galloping along in his horseless chariot; others caught sight of him sitting on his long black cloak as he flew above the fields; and one old grandmother swore blind that the *garabonciás* had charmed the dragon out of the swamp, saddled it and flown off to Mauritania, where it was so hot that the natives died if they didn't slip a piece of dragon's meat under their tongues to keep them cool, and when he got there the wandering scholar intended to slay the dragon, weigh out the meat, and return home one day, heaped with treasure.

The mill was seldom still. The work continued apace, and the wealth of the old miller and the young one alike grew steadily. But Ajándok never again left its confines. She hardly ever spoke. She died within a year, from some mysterious internal disease. Over her grave grows the ever-faithful forget-me-not.

1922

THE TYRANT

DUKE GALEAZZO'S NEW COMMANDER-IN-CHIEF came marching at the head of his army through the triumphal arches of Milan. To welcome their returning soldiers the city had put on display some of the prodigious wealth that had accumulated under the Duke's sagacious rule. The clothes worn by the burghers were worth fortunes. Banners hung from balconies, fluttering proudly in the wind. At banqueting tables across the city the poor were to be Galeazzo's guests.

The King of France's younger daughter, who was passing through on her way to a nunnery in Rome, could only marvel at the unparalleled splendour. But she was sorry that the Duke, whom she had never seen, was not there in person. The gossip was that there was another purpose to her visit, and certainly the French court would have welcomed a connection with the powerful Duke of Milan. But so far he had lived a life of confirmed celibacy, and the chronicles of scandal had never managed to link his name with any sort of bedfellow. It was said that he kept himself aloof from love in order not to be blinded by passion and fall prey to the wiles of a woman.

The procession had now reached the market square, where the crowd was at its greatest and most distinguished. Strange rumours were circulating. Their source was unknown, but everyone was convinced that the day of celebration was about to witness something that had never happened before—the Duke would come down into the city and make his appearance in the square before his triumphant general. Everyone looked forward to his coming with intense curiosity, not least because very few people had any idea what he looked like—not the colour of his hair, or even how old he was. This was because since infancy he had not once, in all his extremely long reign, set foot outside his castle, and had never visited the city he ruled with such great prudence and care.

The Commander-in-Chief, a stout, powerfully built military man, halted his horse before the cathedral. He was still unfamiliar with the customs of the Milanese Court and imagined that the Duke would now ride out to meet him, clap him on the shoulder in front of the assembled crowd and invite him to a princely feast in the castle; the wine would flow until dawn, he and the Duke would be on first-name terms, and they would live as true friends ever after.

A fanfare of trumpets sounded and the Duke's feared personal guard, clad from head to foot in steel, rode into the square. Many of them were huge, grim-faced Hungarians and Germans, men who had no dealings with the citizenry.

The guard fanned out in line. Now everyone was certain that the Duke would step forward, and thousands of eyes focused on one point. But the person they saw was an emaciated old Benedictine, the Duke's Chancellor. The monk made a humble bow, informed the Commander that the Duke was unable to be present, and that he had come instead, as his representative. He would receive his report and give him his instructions for the rest of the day. The arrangement was that that the Commander and the leaders of the mercenaries were to be feasted in the Council House.

The Commander's triumphant face instantly darkened, his head dropped, and he followed the little old man into the Council House. The French King's daughter left the same day.

The banners were rolled up and trundled off, and the flowers given away. People pulled their hats down over their eyes and took no pleasure in the free canteens. The old feeling of hatred that seemed to have been briefly forgotten was back again. If two pairs of eyes met over a raised glass, it was to drink silently to the Duke's demise. If a sixteen-year-old burnt with a nameless ardour, it was because he saw himself as a future tyrannicide, while the older folk simply regretted that the time for that great day was not yet ripe. Once again, the dark shadow of the invisible tyrant lay across the city.

But the Duke, who never knew a single day's rest, and who had never tasted wine in his life, had risen at dawn that morning and worked away at his never-ending tasks of administration. Only for a moment had he glanced out of the window and then, with a small smile of total indifference, he had turned to his Chancellor and observed: "What a lot of people! And every one of them a taxpayer of mine, while I pay taxes to no one … "

His entourage, ageing churchmen grown grey-haired in their studies and black servants alike, had heard this many times before. Not one of them was a Milanese. Galeazzo thought of the people's hatred as a sort of endemic disease that the children of the city carried with them from the cradle and of which not one of them would ever be cured. He knew that—setting aside the blood of conspirators and those sacrificed in his perennial wars of defence—no stain of tyrannical behaviour, however construed, or of cruelty, was attached to his name. And yet there was not one person born in Milan in the last forty years who had not come into the world under the sign of the tyrannicide.

As the huge crowd broke up and despondently drifted away, a rather different sort of ceremony was taking place inside the Court. This was the day when Ippolyto turned sixteen. Ippolyto (known affectionately as Lytto) was a pageboy of noble birth assigned to the Duke's inner cohort of attendants, and the one person, it seemed, for whom Galeazzo felt any personal warmth. To mark the occasion he had presented the boy with a finely worked dagger, which seemed to signify that so far the page had served him with a boyish devotion but from now on he would be expected to defend his lord and master by arms and manly strength. Lytto was thrilled, not so much by the gift itself but by the fact that he had been given it at all, and he kissed the Duke's cold, ring-studded hand with a totally spontaneous ardour. His radiant delight brought a smile to the Duke's lips, and he stroked the boy's head. That action, more than anything else, made it Lytto's happiest hour. He could not remember anyone ever touching his long golden hair so gently before.

The fact was that Ippolyto had come into the world some sixteen years earlier as the child of a guilty love. His mother was a high-ranking lady intimately connected with the Duke's inner circle, and his arrival, it seems, had caused a considerable scandal. No way could be found to conceal the situation from the all-seeing, endlessly gossiping Milanese people, and Galeazzo had decided to have the boy brought up at his side, shielded from prying eyes by a veil of invisibility. The years passed, and his plans for his protégé developed further. He came to see that this young man, who had grown up in the chilling, rarified air of the Court, without parents, a proper home or family tradition, was a real treasure, and he felt that if he could keep him away from the maniacal ideas of the Milanese people during these highly impressionable years and instil in him the disciplined ethos of the court and something of his own rather cold personal charisma, then thoughts of treason would never take hold of him. The boy would become his faithful follower, someone he could trust whatever the circumstances—the sort of adherent he had never previously had.

This scheme, like everything else, he carried out precisely and with great circumspection. Thus from the age of ten little Lytto had set aside his childish toys and spent his days in the Duke's service. He was a serious young man, conscientious by nature, and he performed his duties well. Galeazzo jokingly called him "my walking memory" for his habit of politely drawing his attention to anything he forgot. By now the Duke was beginning to age. Not only was his memory weaker but his body was becoming more susceptible to cold, and Lytto was always to hand with a pillow, a fur coat or a soft footstool for his easily chilled limbs. The strain of too much mental work had made the Duke surprisingly delicate: he could no longer tolerate bright light, or noise, or any kind of slovenliness and dirt; and during his hours of rest only Lytto was allowed near him. With his silent, cat-like tread, his pale young figure that proclaimed both his outer purity and inward innocence, and the comforting gaze of his large eyes with their permanent expression of wonder, his entire person seemed to have been woven from the 'dim religious light' of the holy church itself.

And Galeazzo, who dealt with everyone with the same cool, refined affability, knowing that the fixed smile of ceremonial courtesy would instil a sense of his superhuman, Byzantine power in all who met him, was distinctly more courteous to Lytto than anyone else. He would joke with him every morning, offer him something sweet to eat at midday, and ask him every evening to remember him in his youthful prayers. This gave the impression that of all people Lytto was closest to his heart. In fact Galeazzo behaved in this way simply because he realised that the boy would respond only to gentleness, and in that sense this affectionate treatment differed little from his usual system of government. He felt no greater love for the boy than for anyone else, nor would he permit himself such a love, knowing as he did how dangerous it was for a ruler to have a favourite.

And so this little celebration came to its end. Thereafter the days were filled with a formal, ceremonious monotony. They rose at dawn, to the calling of birds. Everyone had his prescribed duties. The only variety in Lytto's life came through his studies, his tutors being the Duke's learned secretaries. To Galeazzo's great delight, he mastered the Latin language in an astonishingly short time, then the Greek, and became an inspired and enthusiastic student of the classics. These studies made him even more serious than before—what had previously been instinctive in him, his religious piety, his humility and his profound respect for the Duke, were turning into the altogether deeper qualities of a well-educated young man.

A consequence of all this study was that his eyes began to open, and he became aware of things inside himself that he could not understand. For some time now he had been assailed by strange feelings. Galeazzo was a great lover of music, and sitting listening to it at his master's side drove Lytto into a state of irrational agitation and distress. He loved to gaze down from the arched windows of the castle at the city below, lying there silent under the stars in all its unknown, forbidding splendour. He shed tears over the story of Nysus and Euralia. He yearned for some strange and thrilling adventure involving heroic deeds, and was haunted in his dreams by the twin stars of friendship. His loneliness tormented him and served only to deepen his feelings of tenderness towards Galeazzo, the only person (since he was uniformly ignored by the morose inhabitants of the court) who ever took any trouble with him. He never ceased hoping to be able to show some sign of his affection.

And then at last his opportunity came, albeit a melancholy one. As a result of sitting up through the long winter nights, continuous work and a refusal to spare himself, the Duke became ill. He fell prey to nightmares, and his doctors feared for his life. But while everyone else tiptoed round the sickbed in despair, these were wonderful days for Lytto. He was with the patient at all times, cheerfully sacrificing his nights and his beloved studies. He carefully measured out Galeazzo's medicines (a single drop too many might prove fatal), prepared his poultices, and delighted in the fact that the man who had never before depended on anyone now found him indispensable. For the Duke could not bear any sort of woman near him—gossips and poisoners every one! Only from the boy's gentle, love-inspired, woman-like care could he hope for cure. And with time everyone came to feel the same way. Lytto had won limitless power in the curtained sickroom, where Galeazzo's peevishness made it impossible for anyone else to enter. And he wore his new power modestly, the sole, if double-edged, reward for his loving.

In the castle chapel Mass was said for the Duke's recovery. Wearily, unfeelingly, the courtiers counted their beads, while the mercenary guardsmen stood by in grim rows. Lytto went there too for a while, to supplicate the spirit of Divine Love. When the host was raised he summoned all his strength to pray, to appeal to the Presence on the altar from the very bottom of his heart. To add a genuine inwardness to his devotions, he pictured Galeazzo in his mind as already dead and lying stretched out in full armour, surrounded by his bodyguard. Next, his thoughts turned to the Duke's great armchair, in which no one would ever again sit as he had, swaddled in furs. And his whole future life stood before him—without purpose, meaningless and lonely as the sea. He burst into loud sobbing. He saw, in his grief, that without love there could be no true life for him; never again would he enjoy the miraculous taste of Love's feast, for if, in all the endless, empty universe, there were nothing to love, then perhaps God's spirit, that is to say, God's love, might never again hover over him.

He continued to pray through his tears. Soon afterwards, Galeazzo's fever began to abate, and under Lytto's careful nursing he started to recover his strength. On many a bright and sunny winter's afternoon the two would sit together out on the terrace. To the accompaniment of his lyre, the boy would sing deeply poignant Italian love songs, and every now and then Galeazzo's sunken face would turn languidly towards him with an expression that could almost be mistaken for warmth. For all his frailty, the Duke could still tell amusing tales of students, artists and merry widows, none of whom he had ever met in the flesh but whom he knew of with all the hopeless yearning of those who read books. He was now a stooping, heavily wrapped figure. After so much self-neglect, he looked like an old man.

Meanwhile the city down below bathed in the sunlight, in its petty day-to-day business and its seething hatred. For Lytto, it was as if those people did not exist. He inhabited a different, more silent world, almost as lonely as Galeazzo himself. Except that he had someone to love, and that love was enough to link him with all those others down there, dashing about with their own busy loves and hates. Galeazzo had foreseen everything but this: that in time Lytto would come to love him. In that respect, his plan had failed.

Around this time the police arrested Orlondhi and his eleven accomplices in a plot against the tyrant's life. Galeazzo condemned them all to death. Lytto went down to the courtyard in the castle where the executions were to take place. Ever since childhood he had been told of attempts to assassinate the Duke and of those involved being executed, and he had heard the story so often he had come to accept it as normal. Now for the first time he began to wonder why it should be, and who these people were—what sort of deep-dyed criminal would want to end the life of such a benevolent ruler? In considerable trepidation, like someone about to witness a supernatural horror, he dragged himself to a corner of the courtyard and prepared for the worst.

To his extreme surprise, up the steps of the gallows the executioners led twelve fine-looking young men, their heads held high. As they came forward to place their heads on the block, every one of them, by prior agreement, shouted out for all to hear: "Long live freedom! Death to the Tyrant of Milan!"

Profoundly troubled, Lytto made his way as quickly as he could back to his room, his eyes fixed on the ground, like a little boy who feels ashamed of his father and doesn't know why. Having been used since childhood to the fact that other people took no interest in his purely personal feelings, he sought advice from no one. Instead, he locked the door and spread out his books, his little silent senate, on the table. Above all else, he needed to understand why, and how, those twelve young men could plot the murder of an old man and then mount the scaffold, not trembling and downcast, with the distracted, faraway look of assassins being thrust forward at every step into the arms of the devil, but looking around in triumph, their faces radiant, victorious unto death.

His books supplied the answer. The tyrannicide was not a malefactor; rather he was to be ranked with the greatest of heroes. Heroes of this stamp he found in the stories of Pelopidas and his young companions, and of Timoleon, the liberator of Sicily. Livy conjured up for him the proud figure of Mucius Scaevola, pointing with his one remaining arm to the long line of his successors. He even came across the Greek verses that had so inspired the youth of Milan:

When, like Harmodius and Aristogeiton,
I have dispatched the usurper
And made Athenians equal under the law
I shall garland my sword with myrtle leaves.

"But those people were pagans," he reflected. He opened the scriptures and found the book of Judith, who, though but a weak and feeble woman, killed a man and achieved eternal fame. Even the holy and austere Saint Thomas Aquinas—who was himself eventually poisoned by a

French despot—condoned tyrannicide. Ordinary people and philosophers alike agreed that the death of a tyrant was pleasing to God. Soon even Lytto could see that such a person was a pernicious figure, and the enemy of all mankind. But who exactly was a 'tyrant'?

Tacitus and Suetonius told him what he needed to know about the way such people behaved. He gobbled up their pages, scarcely able to wait for long-needed Vengeance to glut itself on the bloody Nero. Now *there* was a tyrant! He set fire to Rome, poisoned his relatives, murdered his mother and put Christians to the torch. He was mad—and more loathsome than any monster. But Galeazzo? How could he be a 'tyrant'. The hideous, bestial image that the word conjured up for Lytto seemed in no way to describe the gentle, refined, almost monkish figure of the Duke. Since childhood, standing at his place behind Galeazzo's chair, Lytto had been present at all the important discussions of affairs of state. He had never taken much interest in them, but he knew all the secrets of the way Milan was governed. And he knew perfectly well that Galeazzo had never perpetrated any of the things those monstrous dictators had. In everything he did as a ruler he had been honourable and humane.

Lytto began to think that there must be some unfathomable, Satanic madness driving the youth of Milan to their death, like moths to the candle.

Then his hand fell on the history of Julius Caesar, that greatest of all rulers, who was slain as a tyrant, in the name of liberty, by his closest friends. Why? Once again everything became confused in his mind.

For many days he carried these burning questions around in his head. But for that very reason he performed his duties all the more punctiliously, and his placid gaze, with its permanent air of wonder, troubled no one. Galeazzo had taught him well: no one could see what lay in the depths of his soul.

One evening they were sitting together in front of the fire. Galeazzo, still convalescent and finding sleep difficult, was ensconced in a large armchair swathed in furs, with Lytto at his feet, lyre in hand. The cosy, dancing half-light would have been enough to stir up memories of younger days and past loves in anyone, but neither of them had any such to call on. However Galeazzo's face was more languid than usual, and he felt at ease with himself. He was enjoying the soft, exquisite singing, the gentle warmth, and the self-indulgent wanderings of the convalescent mind. But above all, he enjoyed having Lytto at his side. He would have protested fiercely against any suggestion that he might love the boy so very much, but he was certainly receptive to everything that was beautiful, and he took real delight in Lytto's noble, upright character as he sat there with his head inclined gracefully over his instrument, and his long hair trailing across his face. Galeazzo felt the need to talk, to embrace the boy with words, the way you might caress a beautiful statue with your eyes.

"I have often thought, young Lytto," he said after a protracted silence, "how strange it is that you never show any desire to get away from this castle, with its permanently cold floors, and that you never seem to be bored beside such a silent person as myself. But you know, I'd be quite happy now to tell you something about my life—not that there is anything to tell … On winter evenings … I always used to sit here in front of the fire … in summer it was in the loggia … I spent my free time in the library. Sometimes I'd watch the guardsmen drilling … and I had so much to do. So much work. I tell you, sometimes I loved just watching the birds taking to the air … and then suddenly the years had all flown away with them, and I was old. Now there's a boring tale for you."

Lytto's fingers trembled on the lyre. No one had ever heard the Duke speak like this before.

"When you were young, my lord, did you never go down into Milan?"

"Never, my boy. If I had, they would have killed me within the hour."

"But what about your bodyguards?"

"Lytto, perhaps you think I am some sort of coward. Well, perhaps. Who can say he truly knows himself? But then, a man who holds the lives of hundreds of thousands of people in his hands, and who would risk everything, is probably exempt from the charge. No, Lytto, I'm not afraid of the assassin's dagger, believe me, nor do I think I shall escape it in the end. What does horrify me is the depth of hatred—you know—the loathsome atmosphere of the hatred of slaves. It would smother me, down there. I begin to wonder if this isn't my greatest achievement, that no man was ever so deeply hated as I am."

The words burst from Lytto's mouth:

"My lord, in the name of all the saints, why do they hate you, who are so good, so virtuous in your life, and always act for the best?"

Galeazzo shrugged his shoulders.

"I don't know, and I'm not really interested. The hatred is in them, not in me. My soul will be found pure on the Day of Judgement. I'm incapable of hatred, myself."

Lytto leapt to his feet.

"My lord, I shall go right now and tell them they are wrong!"

Galeazzo's smile was a sharp as a razor.

"Calm yourself down, my lad, and then we can continue the discussion. No more of these loud words and wild gestures, if you please. Believe an older man, Lytto, there's no helping this hatred until these people change, and change totally, and become like you, and me, and everyone else. The fact is, they hate themselves in me."

"I don't follow you, my lord."

"I'm not surprised, and it isn't important that you should. Every living thing strives for power, Lytto—for domination. Some consciously, some not. The Lord Mayor orders the heads of guilds about, the guildsman lords it over the bootmaker, the bootmaker bullies his apprentices, the apprentice no doubt has younger siblings who torture the cat, the cat torments the mouse, and no doubt even the mouse isn't at the bottom of this ghastly hierarchy. So the mouse hates the cat, the cat hates the children, and everyone hates me, because I am the one with power."

"Is the possession of power worth all the hatred, my lord?"

"I could declaim in poetical tropes, Lytto, how one minute of power is equal to a thousand years of hell. Of course power isn't an end in itself. It is simply an instrument. But it is absolutely necessary."

"Then what is its purpose?"

"Go and ask the meanest beggar in Milan and he will tell you—freedom. That is what glitters at the bottom of the well of their dreams. It's all they worship, and for its sake they will struggle for power, hating whatever power is greater than their own. And yet not one of these people has any idea what freedom is. They are bound by a thousand shackles, these unfortunates: wives, children, relatives, the state of the country, the ceaseless urgings of the body. And everyone is dependent on everyone else. Beat one of them and others will be sure to suffer. If the judge's wife sprains her little finger you can't guarantee that the next day six children won't weep for a father languishing in prison. What they call freedom is a squalid, meaningless lie, because if they did kill me they'd get someone a thousand times worse around their necks. They've got so used to all this they can't live without it. I could even argue that when I do away with these conspirators I do so in their own best interests … but how odd it is, that I should be the only one who knows what freedom means," he added, rising to his feet.

"To be free, Lytto, act as if you were utterly alone—without love, without hatred, without fear and without hope. What man can measure up to that? But what a fine evening this is! Would you play something? We've talked for so long …

"But don't think, Lytto, that I am afraid. I might take myself off to some faraway country for a holiday, where no one would bother me—I tell you, at times I have become very weary of it all and have given thought to such things. But I am a citizen of Milan. Anywhere else I would be a stranger, a guest; not my own master, and no longer free. And if they do succeed in killing me, I'd rather it happened here, at home, where my father and my ancestors met their fate."

"But why, why?"

"Because no one can bear the thought of someone else achieving what he wants for himself from the very bottom of his heart. The free man is a permanent rebuke to others. He reminds them that they are slaves. So keep a tight rein on your passions, Lytto. You are a good, honest lad, with a pleasant face. Perhaps you will never come to understand what you have heard tonight. But if you do, learn from it. Now, isn't it wonderful how I have rattled on this evening? But it's been very agreeable. Now it's time we went to bed. How does the poet put it?

> … *et iam nox umida coelo*
> *Praecipitat, suadentque cadentia sidera somnos.*

> … from the sky damp night
> Sinks to a close, and the setting stars urge sleep.

"Thank you, Lytto, for staying up with me."

And he stroked the boy's hair.

Lytto had not understood very much of what Galeazzo had told him, but as he sat there listening he had been filled with a sense of unspeakable horror. Partly it was a horror of things he could not understand; partly, and more importantly, it was Galeazzo's manner of speaking—his calm, perfectly level tones—that so appalled him. What he could not follow in the words he understood perfectly from the tone of voice—that the man was capable of speaking about other human beings as if he had no personal connection with them—as if he were not himself human.

Nothing more was said until they reached the Duke's bedchamber. There Galeazzo took the candelabra from Lytto and gazed searchingly into his face.

"I've something else to show you, Lytto. I'm sure you have never seen my portrait. I don't normally show it to anyone. But this evening I'm in a good mood, so take a look."

He drew back a curtain and lifted up the candelabra to illuminate the picture.

The painting hung beneath a triple arch. Against a gold background it presented a figure sitting on a tall throne, the body completely enveloped in a dark-green cloak that was so voluminous it covered the steps below and made the face above appear intensely white. The face was horrifying. Lytto instinctively stepped back. It was unquestionably the face of Galeazzo, and yet it was not. With its monstrous calmness, gazing stiffly out at the observer, it seemed no longer the countenance of a human being. The lines were recognisably those of a man, but the expression was of something beyond humanity: certainly not a face to entertain foolish banalities, or indeed one in which anything could be read … and yet it did not seem to conceal any secret. It presented a horrific reality, in which there was nothing to be understood—a face that rejected understanding.

The human forms painted beneath the throne were, in the hierarchical manner of the time, tiny in comparison with the central figure—a vast multitude, all with more or less identical faces, all in some way distorted and seeming to swarm in a kind of restless gloom. Above the throne, the gold background between the two lateral marble arches was interrupted by the unfinished—and truly terrifying—silhouette of two black human figures. The Duke drew the curtains closed.

"Sit down, Lytto. You've gone pale. Pull yourself together," he said. "There's a long story behind this painting. One day, after I had escaped from danger that threatened my actual life, I decided to have my portrait done so that, if I did die, there would be something to hang in the gallery alongside my ancestors. I sent for the most famous painter in Milan and promised him a huge sum of money for the work. He was very happy to take it on. Of course I knew that he would see me through the eyes of the Milanese people and would paint me as I appeared in their vision of hatred. But that didn't bother me. In fact, I was rather pleased. I tell you, it tickled my vanity in those days to be hated by so many people, more than anyone had ever been hated before, and I was delighted that the painter was going to record that loathing for eternity.

"The strange thing about the whole business was that while he was painting me he apparently went mad. He complained of seeing apparitions, he began to prophesy, and he became convinced that he was in the presence of the Antichrist. And one fine day—I've no idea how he came by it—he suddenly ran at me waving a knife in the air. In those days I was still very strong, and my presence of mind has never yet let me down. I picked up a chair and struck him with it. The poor chap was duly executed, and the picture was left, just as you see it, unfinished. Over one of my shoulders there was to be Saint George, the guardian saint of my family, and on the other side Saint Ambrose, the patron saint of Milan. But all you can see are their shadows. So, how do you like the portrait, Lytto?"

"It's very fine, my lord. But it doesn't look like you."

"Good. So mind you don't dream about it! Now off you go. And promise me you will never mention this painting to anyone, or you'll be playing with your life."

Lytto silently raised his hand.

"God bless you, Lytto. You've seen, and heard, some important secrets tonight. But I trust you. You're a good boy."

The next day Galeazzo thought about his talkativeness of the night before with some regret. He had raised a confidant, who might well prove more dangerous than twenty conspirators. Every intimacy we share is a weapon placed in someone else's hands—it lays our bosom open to them. But he did not worry about it for long. He had a strong sense of Lytto's loyalty. He knew the boy had grown up away from all the madness outside. In fact, he began to feel rather pleased about what he had done. The long discussion they had had the previous evening actually completed his earlier project for bringing the boy up—to produce a self-reliant disciple, one who understood his thinking as a ruler, who would serve him on the basis of conscious insight and thus pursue his own interests at the same time.

But in fact Lytto had understood nothing, retaining only the sense of horror that had filled him and the tortured thoughts that continued to trouble his mind. However, it was some consolation that the Duke had taken him so deeply into his confidence that evening. He was certainly pleased that it was he, the simple page-boy, little more than a child, who had been chosen to be trusted with such secrets, and presumably not without reason.

One evening Lytto, kept awake by a combination of his unanswered questions and the general restlessness of young blood, went roaming through the castle. By chance he made his way up to the observatory, where the court astrologer tirelessly practised his strange mumbo-jumbo. When he saw Lytto, his face filled with concern.

"You must pray, young page—pray most diligently for our good lord and master. His star has entered a malign phase and his life is in danger. They tell me you are very attached to him. Is that true?"

"It is," the boy answered, almost shamefacedly.

The astrologer looked at him with real curiosity, as at a miraculous sign or portent.

That night the two of them became quite friendly, although the friendship was rather one-sided. The enthusiasm with which the astrologer sought to initiate him into his not very interesting little technical mysteries left the boy rather cold.

Long after he had become thoroughly bored with the incomprehensible chatter about houses, planets in the ascension, phases of the moon, transitions and periods, he suddenly asked the astrologer:

"What makes the stars move in the sky?"

The man's face filled with reverence.

"What moves the stars is Love, my child. They are attracted to one another as a man is to a woman. They roar across the endless plain of heaven in pursuit of each other."

"Then what can they have to do with the fate of humanity? Surely their own love lives keep them quite busy enough?"

"My boy, my boy, what you haven't grasped is that the same Love also directs humanity. Even as we walk the road of Lesser Love down below, we follow in the steps of the Greater."

"But what about a person who loves no one?"

"There is no such person. Such a person isn't human. He is the Antichrist," the astrologer replied, and made the sign of the cross.

Lytto took his leave and made his way rapidly down from the tower. He was aquiver with excitement. The astrologer's words, filled as they were with superstition, had struck a very deep chord. No one could live without love. So Galeazzo, in his tower of solitude, on his truly horrible throne of 'freedom' … how could he ever stand and look the God of Love in the eye?

Like a fugitive he ran down the dark corridors, between their long lines of columns, his head buzzing with the ancient Italian superstition of the One with the False Face who will appear at the end of the world. Perhaps he had heard of it as a child, or simply knew of it through some ancient folk memory. He sought refuge in ardent prayer, begging for the mercy of enlightenment amidst his terrible doubts, and eventually fell asleep.

That night he had a truly beautiful dream. He and Galeazzo were riding across a wide, sunlit plain. Huge white birds came and sat on their shoulders, and ate scented berries from their hands. Then Galeazzo dismounted, adjusted Lytto's saddle, and looked into his face with anxious concern. "Aren't you tired, Lytto? Are you really not tired, my boy?"

And when he woke next morning, and lay stretching out pleasantly in his bed, he felt that he had solved the riddle. The portrait had simply presented what the mad Milanese painter had dreamt up in his uncomprehending phantasmagoria. And the things Galeazzo had said that evening about power and solitude, those blood-chilling and godless words, were nothing more than the result of a sick and ageing man's momentary bitterness, not to be taken seriously. There was undoubtedly love in Galeazzo's heart, as there was in every man's. His hand was capable of caressing, his eyes of smiling, kindly and gently, like everyone else's. And above all, Galeazzo loved him, the quiet little pageboy. That was the wonderful, the miraculous thing, that such a great man should love such an insignificant child. If the people of Milan ever knew about that, they would instantly throw away their weapons of hatred.

And when he entered the bedchamber next door to rouse the Duke and draw back the curtain around the enormous bed, he smiled at him, intimately, confidently. And, just as he had every other morning since his fever had left him, Galeazzo beckoned Lytto to him, made him sit on the side of the bed, and, in the simple, almost childlike tones of a man only half awake, jested with him about why he had not let him sleep on, when the day had only just broken.

"So what did you dream about, young Lytto?" he asked that morning.

"I'm not telling," the boy replied, blushing.

Mornings like this fully compensated Lytto for his nights of solitary pensiveness.

By now Galeazzo had made a full recovery. The same penetrating, steely look was back in his eye, and he was working as tirelessly as ever. Thinking back over the course of his illness with his usual cool objectivity, he was forced to admit that he had too often let himself go, had on too many occasions been soft-hearted, even sentimental. But at the same time he could not reflect on that illness without seeing, time and again, the boy's faithful figure, leaning solicitously over him or strumming his lyre to drive away his gloomy convalescent thoughts, with the promise of recovery shining in his kindly eye. In truth, whichever way he looked at it, he was now deeply bound to this lad, once his nurse and now his confidant. So when Lytto drew back his bed curtain in the morning, he felt it would now be almost his duty to address him in more intimate terms, and treat him with every kindness. It was now his due.

That idea tormented him endlessly, because for the first time in his life he was in someone's debt and thus in a dependent relationship. So he decided he would reward him with princely generosity and thereby annul the debt to him once and for all.

One day he summoned Lytto before him. He was seated in the Council Chamber in session with his secretaries and his mercenary captains. Lytto bowed low, and Galeazzo made a sign to his Chancellor, who read out the following proclamation:

"We Galeazzo, lawful Duke of Milan, being mindful of the many services rendered to us by our noble page during our recent illness, and further mindful that the highest pleasure of princes is the rewarding of true desert, do hereby acknowledge our noble page as rightful heir to the name and fortune of his late mother the Contessa di Franghipani, now with God, and herewithal entrust the management of his estate to our noble Chancellor, Father Morone, until he be of age; and further, as a mark of our satisfaction with Count Ippolyto di Franghipani, we appoint him henceforth to wait on us in person."

At first Lytto found this great—and quite unexpected—honour overwhelming. He saw it as powerful evidence of the Duke's love, and confirmation that, in his dream, he had indeed solved the mystery that had so vexed him. The tower of solitude and the throne of 'freedom' were no more than a lie—a lie that had now been dispelled, like a fog.

Henceforth he had a new subject for his reveries. Now that he knew himself as Count Franghipani he was determined to be worthy of the ancestral name. His previously formless yearning for romantic, heroic action took on a new intensity. When no one was watching he would pace out the empty, stone-slabbed rooms, with a heavy, solemn stride. He pored over his books with even greater diligence, seeking a suitable model from among the ancient heroes. He gazed lovingly at his little dagger, still his only weapon, and tested its sharpness, trembling in the anticipation of mighty deeds.

But the next morning, when he went to wake Galeazzo, the Duke responded with a haughty toss of the head, murmured, "Thank you, Franghipani," and gestured for him to leave. He never called him Lytto again, treating him instead with the formal courtesy due to a count. The friendship was at an end, and Lytto concluded, despairingly, that legitimising his birth had been neither more nor less than remuneration, salary for a faithful hired servant, and that Galeazzo valued him no more than any of his other salaried attendants. And his old doubts rose up again, with renewed force: could there be any love in this man if he were capable of paying him off in such a cold way for the devotion he had shown? He felt humiliated, that that he had been reduced to the level of a menial. He threw his books in a corner. They could no longer console him. In fact he no longer spent much time thinking. He just gave himself up to his grief.

No one noticed what he was feeling. In fact, it seemed to him that everything was working against him. Finally one day, when he realised that for the third time in a row Galeazzo was not waiting for him to wrap him up in his furs but had entrusted the task to a black footman, all his bitterness welled up inside him and he came to a sudden decision. As soon as he could he slipped out of the room, packed his most essential belongings, secured the dagger in his belt and, stealing along the walls, made his escape from Galeazzo's castle and out into the world.

He did not strike out towards the city. The thought of its unfamiliar atmosphere terrified him. Instead he headed north, across open land, keeping a good distance from the peasants working in the fields. If he came face to face with anyone, even a child, he would draw his dagger, and he took instant fright at the squawking of birds as they fluttered into the air behind his back. Everything was strange and new to him. He felt like a bat driven out of its cave in broad daylight, and he pressed on in inexpressible uncertainty, without aim or direction, already regretting that he had set out at all. Towards twilight he stopped in the centre of an immense field. His legs were shaking. Count Franghipani was afraid—afraid of the falling darkness, afraid of the totally alien landscape.

Suddenly he heard the thudding of hoofs behind him. He was still debating what to do when the horsemen were upon him. They were two Hungarian guards from the Duke's personal entourage.

"We've been looking for you, young man. You're such a fine young fellow the whole troop has been riding around after you. Get yourself home immediately, or there'll be trouble."

Lytto begged them to leave him alone, to let him make his own way in the world. No one needed him at the castle any more.

"Don't talk rubbish. You're the apple of his lordship's eye," said one of the guards.

Lytto stared at him in surprise, then, without a word, allowed them to haul him up onto the saddle and take him home.

Sitting at dinner that evening, the Duke had noticed that Lytto was not at his usual place behind his chair. To his question, where was the young Count Franghipani, no one could offer an answer. He instructed the servants to go and find him. By the time the third course was being served the boy had still not appeared. Galeazzo was overcome by a strange restlessness. He leapt up from the table, seized a torch and set out to look for him in person, with the whole Court following in his wake, calling out "Lytto, Lytto!" in room after room. After a long and fruitless search he finally found someone who had seen the boy leaving the castle through a small gate on the northern side. The Duke immediately ordered his guards to scour the countryside and bring Franghipani back, dead or alive.

He was still pacing up and down the great hall when a tearful and thoroughly demoralised Lytto was brought before him. His face brightened momentarily, then instantly became even more severe than usual. He did not enquire into the reasons for this truancy; he was quite sure they were no more than an adolescent longing for adventure and the urge to wander—nothing of more particular significance. Not for a moment did he doubt his ability to read the boy's state of mind, and he rebuked him thoroughly, in his most coldly domineering manner.

But Lytto was happy. He felt that he had defeated Galeazzo. The Duke's insistence on getting him back had been a silent admission that he loved him.

And so it was. That night Galeazzo did not sleep a wink. He allowed no one anywhere near him, and spent the whole time pacing up and down three large rooms. He had revealed his true feelings to himself. What he had always denied was now incontrovertible—that Lytto mattered to him. He would miss him in his absence, would worry about him. He needed him. In short, he loved him.

He was filled with a rage he would never have believed himself capable of. The tower of solitude, his whole life's work, was tottering. Once you loved someone, what was to stop others laying siege to your heart, and then others again? First the boy, then some friend, then a woman, a mistress, and finally, in the twilight of his life, he too would become the slave of passions, of other people, and an unknown fate—just like all the others he so despised. Once the canker took root inside him he would never be able to tear it out. He would have to nip it in the bud, cauterise the wound, however painfully, before it was too late. He wrestled with himself until dawn, and was ready with his answer. He would send Lytto away. A separation in space and time would do the rest.

So the next day he summoned Lytto back to the Council Chamber, and addressed him as follows:

"Count Franghipani, we commend the study of the French language to your attention. It is true that Latin will suffice for general purposes; but nonetheless, if you are to make yourself fully understood wherever you are, it is essential to speak in the local idiom. It is a courtesy that makes us at home in the country we are visiting. Now, it is our resolve to send you, with a view to developing your talents, to Paris, to a renowned university there to study the disciplines of law and philosophy. As one of our future statesmen, and as a thoughtful person with a tendency to melancholy, you will need both. We confess we have often felt our own lack of a university education, and we desire that you should want for nothing in your adult life and be able, through your studies, to render even greater service to your country. We shall see to it that you have provisions and an escort appropriate to your rank. We have assigned Saint Lawrence's day, which falls three weeks from today, as the date of your departure."

Struck dumb with terror, Lytto uttered not a single word of thanks..

Galeazzo stood up and put his arm around the boy's shoulder.

"I want you to be happy in Paris. Enjoy yourself. Take part in the varied life of a student. Don't hold back on the liquor … And the ladies there, they say, are very good looking. The years will pass, and when you return you will have many tales to tell of your fine and amusing adventures."

In a flash, Lytto saw through Galeazzo's intentions. This too was part of the duel between them. It was Galeazzo's way of freeing himself from the love he felt towards him. He felt sure, from the way Galeazzo's arm had flinched when it touched his shoulder, that a real struggle was going on in the Duke's soul, and he promptly resolved never to submit. Three weeks was a long time. Perhaps he might still manage to get the better of him.

He doubled and redoubled his attentions. His skill was almost magical. And now that he looked at it more closely, it became clear in just how many aspects of palace life he was indispensable. There were so many things, the minutiae of Galeazzo's personal habits and requirements, and where his bits and pieces were kept, that only he understood. It was he who held the keys to Galeazzo's cupboards. The black servants, in contrast, though they danced attendance on the Duke, were clumsy and heavy-handed, which deeply irritated their fastidious master. Only Lytto knew how to tuck him up in bed the way he liked, to pull his boots on without hurting him and pour his drinks with a pleasing, graceful movement of the hand. These and a thousand similar tiny but significant and interconnected details had become associated with his person. The Duke's querulousness seemed to grow from day to day, and his absolute insistence on what he was accustomed to made the ever-attentive Lytto an even more necessary presence, more important than the Chancellor himself. Lytto forgot nothing, was party to everything, and every evening alike the Duke could have had nothing but praise for him.

Then one evening, as Lytto accompanied him to his bedchamber, the Duke's cold hand grasped the boy's face, and he gazed into it, searchingly, for what seemed an age. Lytto withstood the gaze manfully, in a kind of challenge. Galeazzo was the first to relax .

"You're so like your mother!" he said, and his face darkened.

Lytto did not know what to think. He had forgotten how much the Duke despised women.

The next day Galeazzo informed him that he was to be relieved of his personal duties so that he could devote all his time to mastering the French tongue. Lytto studied and studied, but every word of the language, already so harsh and barbaric-sounding to the Italian ear, now seemed even more repulsive and grating. He simply waited for a miracle, desperate to carry out some unprecedented act of heroism that would change everything at the eleventh hour.

Meanwhile something happened that had not occurred in ten years: Galeazzo summoned the highest-born citizens of Milan to the castle to announce his new tax arrangements. He received them in full princely pomp in the Council Chamber, sitting on his throne in a long, dark-green cloak, surrounded by his secretaries in their robes of state, with Lytto, in a crimson doublet, at the foot of the throne. On either side stood serried lines of guards, armed to the teeth. The townspeople were seated at the far end of the hall, the nearest of them a full hundred paces away. In the faces of their proud leaders there was a look of defiant hatred, but their grave formality concealed an element of fear, and when they spoke, their subdued voices were barely audible.

The proposals were duly read out, and no objection was raised. The Duke gestured for the three principal delegates to come forward to receive the new instructions from his hand and make them public.

The three nobles approached. Two of them were old men with beards, in long fur coats. The third was much younger. Lytto was struck by the haggard look on his sharp-featured face. The men knelt before the throne and the Duke held out his hand with the parchment. In that instance the young nobleman leapt to his feet, brandishing a long dagger—no one saw where he drew it from—and let out a blood-curdling scream. And Galeazzo's star trembled.

But before he could land the blow, Lytto, with the unimaginable speed that only the undeveloped frame of a boy would be capable, appeared alongside and with unerring aim plunged his dagger into him. The assassin fell without a sound, and sprawled onto the steps of the throne, writhing grotesquely.

Lytto flung himself down on the bloodstained carpet at Galeazzo's feet, trembling from head to toe with emotion, his head bowed low in full humility—while his heart sang with joy amidst the flood of tears. It had happened. The miracle had happened!

The next moment the line of guards had surrounded the throne and turned their lances on the citizens, who fled the chamber in a stupor of fear. The body was pushed to one side and covered over.

After what seemed an immensely long time, Lytto raised his head and met Galeazzo's gaze. The eyes betrayed nothing. Neither joy at his escape, nor fear of the danger he had been in; neither hatred for his assailant, nor affection for his saviour. Nothing. A complete absence of human expression. Staring stiffly ahead, he remarked, very quietly and very calmly:

"You have a sure hand, Franghipani!"

And that was all. To Lytto, who had expected something rather different after what had just happened, it showed a total want of human understanding. All he felt now was that the miracle had happened in vain. It was too late. He had lost the battle. Galeazzo had killed off the one tie that had bound him to humanity. Filled with loathing, he returned the Duke's cold stare for a moment. Then he suddenly leapt to his feet. He had seen the Face—the face, the vision, that had driven the Milanese painter to madness, the white, expressionless, horrific face on the throne, above the dark-green cloak: Galeazzo's true face, with the mark of the Antichrist on his brow.

After this, Lytto spent no more time thinking. His doubts had all melted away. Now he understood everything. Instead of questions, he was filled with a bleak, dark indifference. He went about his business, fulfilled his duties mechanically, and let the hours and days pass over his head like tall cliffs tumbling down into a deserted valley. The time of his departure was drawing near. His speech was inaudible and his features expressionless—

paralysed by that face, like a small animal hypnotised by the stare of a snake.

Then, just before the date of his departure, something occurred to shake him out of his stupor. The Duke was in council with his secretaries and a document was required. He sent Lytto out to fetch it. Lytto returned, set it down before him, then allowed the hand, whose whiteness had once been such a source of pride to him, to play briefly, with a fine, unconscious grace, on the table. Galeazzo's glance strayed towards it, Lytto noticed the look, and suddenly it was as if he had woken from a dream.

Now he understood exactly why the Duke had said "You have a sure hand, Franghipani". The Duke's diabolical line of thought was clarified in a flash. Galeazzo had thought him capable *of the very same act*: he had been afraid that Lytto would kill him! So little did he believe in love, and so thoroughly had he banished the feeling from his own heart, that he was capable of conceiving such a thought in his head.

The boy's earlier lethargy gave way to a fever of excitement. Once the notion had taken hold in him he could not shake it off. It was with him night and day. He stared at his trembling hand as at some alien object, one on which Fate had laid a terrible summons.

Now his mind was clear: Galeazzo was a tyrant—of all tyrants the most abominable—and the death of such a person was an act pleasing to God. By the end of a feverish night his plans had ripened to certainty, and the next morning he was once again as calm as he had been before temptation troubled his soul. He felt a strange strength in his limbs. His body seemed to him a light, comely thing, as if he were walking on air—as if it were something apart from him, with a will of its own, that might fly off uncontrollably.

At last came the day before Saint Lawrence's. The following day he would have to leave. His project could be deferred no longer. That morning he washed and tended his appearance with particular care. Throughout the day people were struck by his youthful beauty, and many were sorry that he was going. At matins he confessed his sins and received the body of the Lord. In his free time he read Plutarch's portrait of Brutus in the *Parallel Lives*. When darkness fell, he closed the book and made his way up to the castle chapel.

There he prostrated himself before the statue of Saint Ambrose. Words of profound meaning poured from his lips, as if someone were prompting him. On the evening of his great deed, Ippolyto di Franghipani prayed in the following terms:

"Good Bishop Saint Ambrose, you who watch by night over the fate of your people, help me to accomplish the deed attempted by that brave young man from Milan. Grant that I might be courageous and calm in the fateful moment, worthy of my illustrious ancestors, and a faithful emulator of the many glorious heroes of antiquity. It is surely right that it should fall to me to complete what has already cost the lives of so many people. Those brave souls would merely have ended the life of a hated stranger, but I shall sacrifice the one person I have loved above all others. My soul has been washed of its sins, and no selfish desire directs my weapon—I shall act only for the city and for divine Justice. For in the fullness of my heart I believe and confess that the true Christ lives, Christ who, though God himself, suffered for all mankind—while here, Father, is a man who refuses to enter into the sweet and tender ties of love with anyone. I acknowledge that the Tempter has come close to my soul, and I too have built a tower of solitude. But I also love the people of Milan, whom I do not know, as I love all humanity. Shut away in this castle of wickedness, I have felt their blood pulsing through my heart, and I listen to the words of my heart. I have no wish to set myself above the common people, but rather to suffer on my own behalf, on behalf of others, and all mankind. No sense of guilt troubles my soul, because through this deed I shall fulfil the tyrant's own wish. It was he who opened my eyes; who—of his own free will—revealed himself to me in all his impiety and wickedness; who planted the thought of the deed in my mind, and placed the dagger in my hand. It was his way, this non-human in the midst of humanity, of destroying himself, through my agency. Like a scorpion. I know I am your sinful and unworthy servant, weak and fallible, and even as I ask this I do not entirely wish it. But look upon the purity of my intentions, Father, and intercede for me before the Holy Trinity, now and in my hour of death. Amen."

He went back to his room, next to the tyrant's. He waited for everything to go quiet, counting the sweet-tongued bells of Milan as they tolled the hours. He was perfectly calm, and the time passed quickly. At one hour after midnight he rose and went into the tyrant's chamber.

Galeazzo's sleeping face gave away none of his secrets. A little lamp flickered at the foot of his bed. As Lytto came near, he started up and, still half-asleep, enquired:

"Who is it?"

"It is I, Ippolyto di Franghipani," the boy replied calmly.

He drew his dagger, and freed Milan from the tyrant.

1923